Juliet M Sampson

I0670258

Dance Demons

Published by Brolga Publishing Pty Ltd
ABN 46 063 962 443
PO Box 12544
A'Beckett St
Melbourne, VIC, 8006
Australia

email: markzocchi@brolgapublishing.com.au

All rights reserved. No part of this publication may be reproduced, stored in a retrieval system or transmitted in any form or by any means electronic, mechanical, photocopying, recording or otherwise without prior permission from the publisher.

This book is a work of fiction. Names and characters are the product of the author's imagination and any resemblance to actual persons, living or dead, is entirely coincidental.

Copyright © 2016 Juliet M. Sampson

National Library of Australia
Cataloguing-in-Publication entry

Sampson, Juliet M., author.
Dance demons / Juliet M. Sampson.
ISBN: 9781925367263 (paperback)
Subjects: Suspense fiction.
Dewey Number: A823.4

Printed in Australia
Cover design by Wanissa Somsuphangsri
Typesetting by Tara Wyllie

BE PUBLISHED

Publish Through a Successful Publisher. National Distribution, Macmillan & International Distribution to the United Kingdom, North America. Sales Representation to South East Asia
Email: markzocchi@brolgapublishing.com.au

Dance Demons

Love, loss and the rhythm of the soul

JULIET M. SAMPSON

About the author

Juliet M. Sampson is an international author of novels *Bon Voyage!* and *Behind the Mask*. Storytelling has always been part of her life. In her other profession as a teacher, she continues to share this love.

Juliet has always been exposed to the world of dance, learning styles of jazz, ballet and tap. Cha Cha, Rumba, Jive and Samba, the world of Latin dance has recently been introduced to her and Juliet has her bronze and silver Latin medals and gold Cha Cha. A passion for dance has inspired her writing. She is currently writing her fourth novel.

To find out more, visit Juliet's website:
http://www.julietmsampson.com.au

For my Mum, Dad, Grandpa
and fellow dancers all over the world.
And to Vicki, Dulcie and Cheryl
for sharing their love of dance.

Prologue

Dance floor - July 2015

'Don't say a word,' Anton whispered, placing his finger to his lips.

The two dancers gently swayed in the middle of the dance floor. A bright beam from the fluorescent light caught Stephanie's figure, casting a delicate shadow upon the wooden floorboards.

Listening to the music, Stephanie allowed Anton to lead her movements. Rotating her hips in time with his, she danced the Salsa steps. The movements were easy and loose, and although swaying her hips was something she was once afraid of, this was no longer the case.

'Stephanie, I love the way you move your hips.'

'Thanks.' She smiled shyly. 'Anton … I need to ask you something. Are you …'

'Am I what?'

'Are you … interested in me at all, like, romantically?'

'Steph … I'm your dance teacher. I'm much older than you.'

'But I've been in a relationship with an older guy before.'

'Stephanie … let's just concentrate on the steps.'

Stephanie sighed. Anton did not understand what she had been dealing with, the recent loss of Andrew and the struggle to get out of bed every morning. Dancing with him had now become her life.

'But Anton ... ' she muttered as he continued to dance. Her weary body gently swayed as he led her into the next step. Trying to catch his gaze she lost balance and the sole of her shoe slipped against the floor.

'Ah!' she shrieked.

'What happened? Did you hurt yourself?'

'My foot ... ' She leaned over to rub her ankle.

Anton placed his hand on her shoulder. Stephanie stared wildly into his eyes.

'Steph ... some things are just not meant to be,' he said quietly as he offered her his other hand.

Stephanie tried to fight back the hot tears forming in her eyes. Gently dropping a kiss on her forehead, Anton then led her off the dance floor.

'Sit down and rest that foot. I've got something to help you,' Anton offered. Turning his back, he switched off the dance music and left the room.

Looking down at her feet she noticed her toes had changed colour as the black straps dug deeper into her soft skin. Taking off her dance shoes, the colour seeped back into her feet. A teardrop landed on her lips as a salty taste entered her mouth. Wiping her eyes, the black mascara smudged onto her hands.

Pins and needles ran up the back of Stephanie's legs. She looked over at the staircase, wondering if she should make an exit. Struggling to stand, she took a deep breath and faced the stairs. Stephanie paused to rub her aching leg. She gasped. Someone was breathing on the back of her neck.

'Anton, is that you?'

'You look in pain.'

Someone pushed her back onto the couch. Stephanie looked up to see Anton standing over her. He held out a glass of water.

'I didn't mean to scare you. Here, take this.'

'What's this?' she hesitated. Tiny silver specks started to appear in front of her eyes.

'Trust me, just take it! The pain will go away.'

Anton handed Stephanie a white tablet. Her hand trembled as she accepted his offer.

'Go on. What are you waiting for?'

Closing her eyes, she allowed the tablet to slip down her throat.

Chapter One

November 2014

Stephanie breathed a sigh of relief as she walked out of her final exam. She had breezed through the multiple choice section but had struggled with writing the essay.

'All over till next year!' Nicole chirped.

'Thank goodness,' groaned Stephanie.

'I started to panic a little when I read the essay topic. I need good marks in English. I know what my parents will say. "How did you go?" Dad desperately wants me to study Law ... another year before I can do that.'

Mrs Mandell was walking towards them. Stephanie noticed her long boots that clunked along the pathway. She was a trendy teacher who moved with the times.

'Has the exam finished already?'

'Sure has!' Nicole beamed.

'So, how was it?'

'Multiple choice was pretty straight forward but the essay question was hard.'

'What was it?' Mrs Mandell's nostrils flared.

Nicole folded her arms. 'It was about underage drinking.'

'Oh really … I must go and have a chat to Mrs Rondon and hear what she thought about the paper – '

'Mrs Oxford briefly spoke about that topic in Legal Studies,' Stephanie interrupted.

'They may have chosen the question because of the recent debate in the news,' Mrs Mandell said with a deep sigh. 'I guess the board wants to keep up with current issues.'

The school bell rang, doors opened and students in blue and white uniforms carrying books spilled out into the school ground.

'I better get going, girls. I'm not sure if I'll see you again. Have a good break. You'll be head of the school next year, exciting!'

'I know, right,' said Nicole proudly.

'Enjoy your break too, Mrs Mandel. See you next year,' Stephanie said politely.

The pathway became crowded as groups of students rushed past. Blue and white checks everywhere. The grey buildings towered over the girls as they headed for the locker room to collect their school bags.

'We learn more about these issues in magazines. I read an article about underage drinking – so many kids our age do it. I bet we'll get invited to some parties next year.' Nicole whispered to Stephanie.

'Mmm, I guess we will but I'm not really into drinking. I have one occasionally with my parents and Andrew doesn't drink around me, only with his mates.'

Nicole grinned. 'Yeah, I like Vodka Cruisers but my parents only let me drink on special occasions.'

Stephanie sighed. She was looking forward to the school holidays and enjoying Andrew's company.

'I wonder if I'll be in Lizzy's class next year,' Nicole said as she looked over at a group of girls.

'Lizzy Butell?'

'Yes, Lizzy's the school captain next year. I'd like to get to know her.'

'Yeah … ' replied Stephanie with little interest.

Nicole smiled at the girls as they walked past. 'Steph, I think they looked my way – '

'I didn't see Jan or Jeanette in the exam,' Stephanie interrupted.

'Neither.'

'There must have been at least 100 people in there,' Stephanie said as they approached the lockers.

'At least, I think I may give Jan a call when I get home. See what she thought of the exam. I know she was dreading it,' Nicole groaned.

Stephanie rolled her eyes. 'So was I.' She slammed the locker door and grabbed her school bag heading for the gate.

'Slow down, Stephanie!' Nicole wheezed. 'I can't keep up!'

'Is your sister picking you up?' Stephanie asked as they hurried through the gate.

'She said she would. It's handy having an older sister. Guess Andrew's picking you up?' Nicole looked at her watch, still trying to catch her breath.

'Yeah, he is.'

'You're so lucky to have him. I wish I had a boyfriend. But I don't think it would be easy.'

'What do you mean?'

'My dad doesn't want me to date,' Nicole groaned. 'I have to finish school first.'

'Andrew's finished school, my parents like that fact. You'll find someone when the time's right.'

'Guess so,' Nicole nodded. 'Anyway, you must be excited?'

'You mean about my birthday?' Stephanie smiled.

'Well, it's tomorrow. What do you have planned?'

'It's just my seventeenth, so next year will be the big one. I'm just going to have lunch with my parents and Andrew.'

'That's nice.' Nicole leaned against the fence. 'I've got my eighteenth planned already and I'm going to ask some of the guys from school. Dad will just have to get over that. I really want to ask Jim. I think he would like him. He's Greek too.'

Stephanie smiled. She loved the way Nicole always planned in advance.

'I overheard him telling the guys he is trying out for the soccer team. Andrew plays soccer?'

'Yeah, he does.'

'I might have to come and watch. When I get home I have to remember to pluck my eyebrows. I don't want them getting too thick. Greeks have a reputation of being hairy. I don't want that happening to me. My sister is so conscious of it, she plucks her eyebrows monthly, you know,' Nicole said before leaning in closer towards Stephanie. 'Yours are getting a bit thick …'

'Yeah, I don't like them really thin. I like a natural look,' Stephanie said as she brushed her finger across them.

'Ha, me too. I hate it when it looks like people have drawn them on their face. I heard a story about a lady who shaved hers off. They never grew back so she had to draw them on all the time.'

'That's scary.'

'I know. Anyway, after next year I'm going to dye my hair.' Nicole started to wind her long hair around her finger. 'I'm sick of this jet black colour I want streaks of light brown. I'll be eighteen then and Dad won't be able to freak out.'

'I like your dark hair.' Stephanie stood back and admired her friend.

'I want a change but I just have to be patient,' Nicole sighed. 'I'm looking forward to the holidays. There's so much I want to do.'

Stephanie nodded. 'I know what you mean.'

'How's the library job going?'

'Yeah, I really love it.'

Nicole gave her a nudge. 'So, that's an option when you finish school?'

'It's an idea. I've enjoyed my shifts.'

Nicole grabbed the lip balm from her pocket and smothered it onto her cracked lips. 'Want some?'

'No thanks.'

'So what are the people like at the library? Any male staff?'

'Do you remember Emma? She used to go here.'

'Vaguely.'

'She got me the shifts, we've become good friends. And then there's Ally, my supervisor.'

'Any males?'

'No male staff,' Stephanie laughed.

'Just asking!' Nicole started to laugh too.

A car turned the corner and travelled in their direction.

'Here she is. I'll call you tomorrow and wish you happy birthday.'

Giving Steph a quick hug, Nicole collected her school bag and headed for the car. She waved out the window as her sister honked the horn.

Stephanie sighed. She admired the way Nicole lived her life. *Geez, it must be hard growing up in a strict Greek family,* she thought.

Stephanie knew she had a good relationship with her parents and her mother acted like a friend. They shared many deep and meaningful conversations. But Andrew was her best friend. She knew everything about him and had grown to love him. He texted her every morning and she saw him most nights. He was the guy for her. She could see his car in the distance.

'How did it go?' Andrew asked as Stephanie climbed into the car.

'Glad it's over. Multiple choice was okay but the essay question was a different story.'

Andrew groaned. 'So glad I've finished school.'

'Thanks,' Stephanie said, rolling her eyes.

'Sorry, you only have next year to go. It's holidays now.'

Stephanie sighed. 'Yeah, thank goodness.'

'Well, it's true. You can throw those study books out the window.'

'You know I can't do that.'

'I bet you wished you could!' Andrew started to laugh.

Stephanie smiled. He was right - if she did not have to go back next year, she gladly wouldn't.

'And your day?'

'Busy. I'll have to drop you home and go straight to work.'

'You got the late shift today?'

'Yeah, unfortunately. And the morning shift. That's why I'll be late for lunch tomorrow.'

'I know, you told me.'

Andrew turned to face Stephanie. 'I know it's your birthday and I'll be there to celebrate properly but we are doing something special the next day. A big surprise.'

'I know.' She smiled in approval. Andrew never let her down.

'Steph, you're gonna love it. I don't know how I've managed to keep it a secret this long, actually.'

'Can't you just tell me already?'

'No way, and spoil it now?'

'Pleeeeeease?'

'Don't look at me with your puppy dog eyes. It's a surprise.'

Stephanie started to giggle.

'Made you laugh!'

The car arrived at the front of her house.

'Here we are.'

Stephanie leaned over and kissed Andrew on the lips. She had never had a connection like this with anyone before.

'See you soon. I love you.'

'Love you too, Steph.'

Stephanie waved goodbye to Andrew as he reversed the car out of the drive.

Tomorrow was her birthday and she needed to get excited about that. The pressure of the exam was behind her now and she had so many things to look forward to.

Chapter Two

Stephanie relaxed back into her chair, admiring the seaside view. The sun's rays sparkled on the still water.

'School's finished now,' her mother whispered across the table. 'You can have some fun. Spend time with Andrew.'

Stephanie glanced at her watch, wondering where Andrew was. Twenty minutes ago her parents had sung happy birthday. She finished the last mouthful of chocolate cake.

'I've asked the waiter to save Andrew a piece,' her mother said.

'Thanks, he shouldn't be long. He knew I was having a cake but said not to wait for him. He didn't know when he would be finishing work. He'll celebrate with me later.'

Stephanie glanced at her watch again, hoping he would arrive soon. He had not texted her this morning which was strange.

'Stephanie, you look stunning,' said a familiar voice.

Stephanie looked up to see Andrew standing over her smiling.

'Happy birthday,' he cooed and kissed her gently on the cheek.

Stephanie smiled. Andrew always made her feel good.

'Here, Andrew, take my seat.' Stephanie's father moved to another chair at the table.

'I'm sorry I couldn't get here any earlier. A lady at the gym collapsed and I had to call the ambulance.'

'Is she okay?' Stephanie asked.

'I'm not sure I just saw the ambulance arrive,' Andrew said as he hung his jacket over the back of his chair. 'Hey, I'm sorry I didn't get a chance to text you this morning. I feel bad.'

'Don't at all, it doesn't matter. We're celebrating tomorrow night anyway.'

'But your birthday is today.' Andrew reached into his gym bag and placed a blue box with a silver ribbon on it in front of Stephanie. 'This is for you.'

Stephanie gasped. 'Andrew!' Taking a deep breath she untied the ribbon and removed the lid. 'Wow. I love this! Thank you.'

'Can I have a look?' her mother asked. 'What did he give you?'

'Mum, you can have a closer look in a minute.'

The silver chain caught the light as Stephanie let Andrew attach the clasp of her bracelet.

'There you go, show your mum.'

'That's beautiful! You really do spoil her.'

Andrew gazed into Stephanie's eyes. 'We've been going out for a while now. How long has it been?'

He gave her a soft look of affection. Stephanie nodded in response. She loved it when he looked at her in this way.

'We started dating around the end of Year 10. I remember you walking over and asking me if there was a spare seat at my table.' Andrew reached for Stephanie's hand. 'I didn't know what you were thinking, I didn't know if you would like me,' he muttered. 'I had spoken to a few girls but, Steph, there was just something about you.'

Stephanie gave a deep sigh. 'Andrew, please, don't embarrass me.'

'What? It's true. I knew you were the one for me,' he said softly as he squeezed her hand.

'Look at you two love birds.' Jane admired the young couple.

'Mum ...' Stephanie glanced at the table next to them. 'We're in a restaurant, other people may hear you – '

'Don't embarrass them, Jane,' her father interrupted.

'They're so sweet. Look at them, Larry. Just like the two of us when we were dating.'

Larry nodded and placed his hand on Jane's. 'Will we order some coffees? Here, Andrew, have something to eat. We saved you some birthday cake.'

Andrew started to chuckle. 'I love the way you change the subject, Larry.'

'Andrew!' Stephanie rolled her eyes.

'Larry and I are good mates. I'm fine for food, thanks. I had a big breakfast before work.' He looked over at Stephanie giving her a wink. She gave his hand a gentle squeeze.

'Was it busy at the gym this morning?' Jane asked.

Andrew nodded. 'It can be sometimes, especially on Saturdays – '

'I really need to go to the gym,' Jane interrupted. 'I want Stephanie to come with me but since she's been working at the library she never seems to have much time to herself.'

'I know the feeling,' Andrew laughed. 'You have to book her a long time in advance. I'm old news.'

Stephanie smiled and rolled her eyes.

'Just kidding,' Andrew added with a laugh.

'I'm working more shifts starting on Monday,' Stephanie said. 'Remember, it was you guys who suggested I get a summer job.'

'Yes we did,' her mother nodded. 'Anyway, I think you two should go and spend some time together. We'll see you later in the day.'

'Sounds good to me,' chirped Andrew as he got up from his chair. He reached out his hand to shake Larry's and kissed Jane on the cheek.

'Bye, Mum and Dad. Thanks for all this.'

'You're welcome, love. Now go and enjoy yourself.'

'I know where I'm going to take Stephanie, for a walk along the beach,' Andrew said, placing his hand on her shoulder.

The two lovers walked hand in hand along the foreshore. The warmth of the blazing sun was on Stephanie's back. The smell of seaweed wafted in the air. Her gaze was drawn to the ripples in the water. She felt at peace as she watched the water gently wash over the rocks. There was no other place that she would rather be.

'What a beautiful place this is. I love the sea.'

Andrew had stopped and was admiring the view. He rested his arm across Stephanie's shoulders as she snuggled in closer to his muscular body. Brushing his hand over her silky hair, he turned to gaze into her blue eyes. She squinted and wished she had worn her sunglasses.

'You're too gorgeous, Stephanie. I love it when you do that.'

Stephanie knew she was the only woman for Andrew even though he was always in the spotlight on the soccer ground with women craving his attention.

'Watch out!' Andrew shouted.

Stephanie lost her balance and fell into Andrew's arms as two barking dogs ran passed them.

'I love dogs and all but why don't people put them on leads? Good thing I was here to catch you.' Wrapping his arm around Stephanie, they made their way to a wooden bench.

Andrew brushed Stephanie's long brown hair back behind her ear and leaned in closer. She always felt safe with Andrew.

'I'm excited about the future, Steph. One more year and you'll be finished school.' He gently kissed the back of her soft hand.

Andrew was charming. Whenever he looked at Stephanie with his sparkling brown eyes, butterflies formed in her stomach instantly.

'I'm excited about the future too. We have so much to look forward to.'

Giving Stephanie a wink, he started to laugh and stroke her back.

'That feels so good.'

'Mmm, I worry about your back. You're always sitting at the computer in the library. Moving around a bit more would be good for it, I reckon. Have you thought about getting back into dancing?'

'I don't have time for that. I've not danced for years. In the library I do move around returning the books to the shelves.'

Andrew sighed. 'Still, that's not enough.'

The moment was interrupted as a short muscular guy placed his hands on Andrew's shoulders.

'Webb, man! You coming out with the boys tonight?'

'Ah, Wayne, how are ya? I didn't see you there, mate.'

'Ha, yeah, same old. Just running about, keeping the training up. So are you coming tonight or what?'

Andrew looked at Stephanie as if to get her approval. She gave him a half smile and then looked away.

'It's Steph's birthday today.'

'Oh, happy birthday! Hope Webbo's spoilt ya?'

'Sure did ...' Stephanie said as she held out her wrist. The silver bracelet sparkled in the sunlight.

'Rad!'

'Andrew, go for a drink with the boys tonight,' said Steph. 'We're having dinner tomorrow night.'

Andrew reached for Stephanie's hand. 'Are you sure?'

'Yeah, go.'

Wayne gently slapped Andrew's back. 'Great. I'll pick you up at eight, man.'

'Thanks, mate.'

Wayne continued to jog along the path. There was something about Wayne that Stephanie did not like. He seemed to be the group clown.

Stephanie and Andrew had encouraged Wayne to date Jan but she had only lasted one week. Jan had said she preferred footballers to soccer players but Stephanie had thought there was more to the story.

'Okay, so, tomorrow night. I'll pick you up at seven for the big surprise. I love you.' He gently kissed her lips.

Stephanie snuggled into Andrew as he wrapped his arm around her. It was beginning to get windy and Stephanie's hair was blowing into her face.

'You're shivering?'

'I should have brought my jacket. It's freezing now.'

Andrew held her closer. 'I know, I can see goosebumps on your arms. Let's go home.'

This was Stephanie's last memory of Andrew.

Chapter Three

Stephanie was watching the television when the phone rang. Her mother answered the call.

'Stephanie, there's ... there's something I need to tell you,' she said sadly.

'What ... what's happened?' she said without averting her eyes from the television.

'It's Andrew. He ... he was in an accident last night ...'

Stephanie turned sharply to look at her mother. Her stomach dropped.

'He was hit by a car, Steph. I'm ... I'm so sorry, darling. He didn't make it ...'

'What ...' Water suddenly brimmed in Steph's eyes. 'But ... he was at my birthday celebration yesterday ...' Hot tears rolled down her cheeks.

'Oh, Steph ... ' cried her mother as she wrapped her arms tightly around her daughter.

Steph shook in her mother's arms. She began to sob uncontrollably.

'I ... I can't believe it. How did it happen?'

'I spoke to Luke on the phone. Patricia was too upset to talk. Andrew had been at a bar with some of his mates. When they left to walk home … a car hit him,' she sniffed. 'Oh, darling, I don't know what to say …'

Stephanie continued to cry in the arms of her mother.

'Why … why has this happened?' she whispered.

Her mother gently rocked Stephanie in her arms, 'I wish I could explain, love … '

The week before the funeral dragged. Stephanie's eyes were swollen for days from endless tears. She had not felt like leaving the house and no longer wanted to see the sunshine. Most of the time she hid in the dark and safety of her bedroom.

Stephanie woke to a knock on her bedroom door.

'Stephanie, we don't have long. Come and have your breakfast.'

Breakfast was a struggle as she took tiny bites into her buttery piece of toast.

'Are you going to finish eating that, love? Probably best you should.'

Stephanie stared at her toast. 'I'm not that hungry.'

Her mother gave a half smile. 'Okay. I'll clean up. You get ready.'

Stephanie washed her hands under the tap and then made her way to the bedroom. Pulling her black dress over her head, she looked into the mirror. The silver bracelet was a big contrast to her black dress. She gazed at her image, she wanted to wear the bracelet for Andrew. It was the last gift he gave her.

'Are you ready, darling?' her mother asked.

'Yes, I'm ready.'

'Okay, we're leaving in ten minutes.'

'Can we go straight in?' Stephanie asked. 'I don't want to stand out the front.'

'Sure, love,' replied her mother sympathetically.

The sun shining through the stained glass windows created a rainbow of colours on Stephanie's black dress as she entered the church with her parents.

'Let's sit up the front with Andrew's parents,' her mother suggested. 'I can see Patricia over there.'

Avoiding eye contact with others, Stephanie placed her lanky body onto the wooden pew and stared at the floor. A musky smell rose from the candles that surrounded a large black coffin with golden handles.

Stephanie looked up. She was devastated to see Andrew's coffin. He had walked along the beach with her last week and now he was dead.

Grabbing a tissue from her bag, she wiped a tear that rolled down her cheek. *Why Andrew?* She thought. Holding the tissue tightly in the palm of her hand, she shut her eyes and listened to the sombre organ music that echoed around the church.

'We are gathered here today to celebrate the life of Andrew John Webb.'

Stephanie opened her eyes to see an elderly man standing in front of the congregation.

'Andrew was full of life and loved his parents dearly.'

Another tear rolled down her cheek.

'Andrew had many friends and was well respected amongst his peers. He loved soccer and won many awards. Andrew worked hard to reach his goals and to fulfill his dreams.'

Dreams, Stephanie thought. *My dreams have been smashed to pieces. Shattered like a glass bottle that has been thrown onto the floor.*

'Long live his memory in the hearts of all he loved. Please

reflect as we listen to the song "I Will Always Love You", chosen by Andrew's parents.'

The sweet voice of the female singer echoed around the church.

'And I will always love you ...'

Stephanie shut her eyes and listened.

'Sweet memories are all I'm taking with me ...'

She sighed deeply. *How can Andrew be dead?* she thought. *Why is this happening?* She could see an image of them walking along the beach. Andrew was holding her hand.

'I'll always love you ...'

The song finished.

The priest stood up. 'Heavenly Father, please bless us today as we meet in friendship and love. Today and always we know in our own hearts that we may walk through the valley of the shadow of death and know Lord that you are with us to guide and protect us. Amen. Now we have Stephanie to do a reading.'

The wooden floorboards creaked under her feet as she made her way to the lectern. Stephanie looked out at the people as she positioned herself in front of the microphone.

'Psalm 23, The Lord is my Shepherd.

A Psalm of David.

The Lord is my Shepherd; I shall not want. He makes me to lie down in green pastures; He leads me beside the still waters. He restores my soul; He leads me in the paths of righteousness For His name's sake. Yea, though I walk through the valley of the shadow of death, I will fear no evil; For You are with me; Your rod and Your staff, they comfort me. You prepare a table before me in the presence of my enemies; You anoint my head with oil; My cup runs over. Surely goodness and mercy shall follow me all the days of my life; And I will dwell in the house of the Lord Forever.'

A tear dropped onto the paper as she breathed through her nose. Her hand trembled as she made her way past the coffin and to her seat. A bunch of red roses rested on the coffin next to a photo of Andrew. His haunting eyes looked at Stephanie.

'Thank you, Stephanie. I believe Wayne is now going to speak.'

Wayne walked to the front of the church.

As he stood behind the lectern, Wayne looked at the congregation. He could barely reach the microphone but tried to stand up tall. Stephanie wiped her eyes.

'Andrew was a mate who never let you down. A talented sportsman and a loyal friend. We met through soccer. I admired his skills and strength. Not only was he a great player but he was my best mate.' Wayne sniffed into the microphone his voice became shaky. 'He was always there for me right through to the night of his death.' Wayne looked at Stephanie. 'I'll always cherish the good times we had. He made me laugh and believed in me. Andrew encouraged me not to live in fear just to reach for my dreams … Even though I feel so sad, I know Webbo wouldn't want me to be. I'll never forget you, mate … You were one in a million.'

'Thank you, Wayne, we'll now have a few minutes silence to reflect on the life of Andrew.'

A screen on one side of the church displayed photos of Andrew that represented times in his life; family, friends, high school, soccer, the day he got his car and of course, ones with Stephanie.

Stephanie's eyes watered and tears began to follow.

'Now Andrew is walking with God. His memory will live forever. I have been asked to read this piece on behalf of Andrew's family.

In loving memory of Andrew John Webb.

Cherished Friend.

Once in a long while, someone special walks into your life and really makes a difference. He takes the time to show you in so many little ways that you matter. He sees and hears the worst in you but doesn't walk away. In fact, he may care more about you. His heart breaks with yours, his tears fall with yours, his laughter is shared with yours. He will be sadly missed. Rest in Peace, Andrew.'

The melancholy music resonated around the church. Six males in black suits stood, three on either side of the coffin. Resting it on their shoulders, they then began to walk down the aisle.

Grief sat in Stephanie's stomach as a sharp pain stabbed her heart. The large coffin was carried past their row. Stephanie spotted three familiar faces. Nicole, Jan and Jeanette. Her friends were wiping their weepy eyes.

'Mum,' she sobbed. 'We have to go. I can't stay any longer.'

'Of course, love. Here's the key to the car. Your father and I will just say a few words to Patricia and Luke before we leave.'

Chapter Four

Stephanie was glad it was all over. Her bedroom was her safe haven protecting her from the outside world. Life continued to fade into nothing.

Day after day, week after week, Stephanie sat on her bed and stared at the cream walls. Her eyes watered and the tears rolled down her cheeks. The door of her room remained shut as she pretended to read. The greyness in her mind was becoming darker. Placing her watch next to her ear, she focused on the ticking sound.

Tick, tick, tick.

Something was ready to explode inside her.

She made her way over to the window and peered out through the tiny crack in the curtain. The grey sky outside did not look very inviting but she needed to get out of her room. Zipping up her jacket she quietly left the house.

Stephanie gazed into the cloudy sky. The funeral had been one of the worst days of her life and now she was left to face the world alone. She listened to the waves crashing.

My dreams have been ripped to pieces, she thought. *How could this happen to me?*

This familiar place was so different now. On her birthday the two lovers had enjoyed the sunshine and Andrew had whispered sweet words of romance into her ear. Today it was a cold, quiet place with hardly a person in sight.

Stephanie watched the murky dark blue water crashing against the jagged rocks. The wind howled as she wiped her eyes. Bits of her hair blew all over the place. The soft wool of her grey knitted scarf provided warmth and comfort as she continued to walk along the foreshore.

The heels of her long black boots clanked as they hit the hard cement. Step by step she walked on what seemed an endless path. Where was she heading? She was not sure.

Stephanie's blue eyes met with the wooden bench where she and Andrew had sat when discussing the future. This dream was lost. Her eyes began to water and then they began to sting. Her stomach began to rumble as she had eaten very little in the last few days. Taking a deep breath, she sat on the bench and watched the black-feathered birds with their long necks in the water.

Stephanie could taste salt in her mouth. Rubbing her hands together, the thought of death entered her mind. Maybe if she jumped into the water the waves would crash over her and that could be the end?

Water droplets started to drizzle down her jacket. The rain did not bother her. It just reflected her mood. This was it. This was the end. All she needed to do was stand on the edge and jump.

Fighting back tears, she stood up. Looking into the sky, she noticed the ominous dark clouds. The rain became heavier and the waves grew bigger. Flipping her scarf over her shoulder, step by step, she walked along the wooden pier keeping her focus on the rough water. The wind howled. Taking another deep breath, she knew there were only metres to walk.

The squawking white birds flew high above her struggling against the strong current of the wild wind.

Buzzzzzzz!

Stephanie stopped. Reaching into her pocket, she pulled out the phone. Hesitant, she pushed the button and answered the unknown number.

'Hi, Steph.'

She recognised the voice.

'It's Emma. Just wanted to ask you to dinner tonight. I know it's late notice.'

Stephanie paused. A tear rolled down her cheek.

'Steph ... are you there?'

'Yeah, sorry Em. What time were you thinking?'

'Is seven okay?'

'Yeah, sure. I'll see you then.'

She placed her phone back in her pocket. The edge of the pier was five more steps. The wind pulled at her wet clothes, edging her closer as the rain soaked her jacket. She took two steps forward. *Is this it? No ...* she thought.

Stephanie quickly turned her back on the water and began to walk. She wanted to leave the beach and return home.

As she headed through the park, her steps turned into a run. The water splashed onto her boots as her heels crushed the soggy grass. As she waited to cross the esplanade from the beach, she touched her damp hair. The movement of the passing cars made her feel dizzy but she could not stop, she needed to keep going. A brief pause in the traffic allowed her to take her chance and she continued to run. Stephanie made it to the other side. Car beams lit the wet road. It was not much further to walk.

Turning the corner, she was now only metres away from her front door. The cream brick building was in sight. Stephanie was nearly there. *Home, sweet home,* she thought.

Frantically, she reached into the pocket of her jeans for her key as she approached the front door.. She pushed hard against the stubborn, wooden door as the brass key clicked. Suddenly, she collapsed.

'She's awake.' Emma was standing next to Stephanie's bed. A long plastic tube hung from Stephanie's arm and a bracelet with her name on it was tied around her wrist.

'Where am I?' she asked.

The next familiar voice was her mother's. 'You're in hospital, darling. You collapsed.'

'Collapsed?' Stephanie could not remember.

'Don't speak, just rest.' Her mother held her hand. 'When I arrived home from work I saw you in the doorway and called the ambulance. They have now admitted you to the ward for further investigation. They assure me at this stage everything seems fine,' she huffed. 'We're hoping you'll be able to leave tomorrow. Now get some rest, love.' She kissed her daughter on the cheek. 'You can spend some time with Emma. We'll be back tomorrow. Visiting hours are nearly over. Love you.'

'Thanks, Mum. See you, Dad.'

Her parents left the room.

Emma moved closer to the bed. 'I was shocked to hear you were in hospital. We'd just been chatting on the phone. I was about to start cooking the dinner when your mother called. To be honest, Steph, I'm pretty worried about you. You've been on my mind a lot.'

Stephanie looked down, not wanting to make eye contact.

'Anyway, where were you before you collapsed?'

'Walking along the beach.'

Emma frowned. 'But the weather was terrible? You'll get sick doing that. And yes, I know I sound like your mother, but it's only 'cause I care.'

Stephanie groaned. 'I was just … feeling sad. I miss Andrew. It feels like he has been gone forever. I wanted to go to the beach.' Her eyes got watery.

'Ohhh, don't cry. I wish I could give you a hug. You look uncomfortable in that hospital bed. Next time you're feeling sad please call me. I'll be over straight away.'

Stephanie wanted to talk more to Emma about the whole experience, how the phone call had changed her mind about jumping but something was holding her back.

Stephanie looked away. Her eyes were drawn to a machine high up on a shelf. 'What's that machine?' she asked.

'I think it's a heart monitor. Not sure, I'm not a doctor or nurse. Once I saw one of those on a medical documentary. I remember watching the black screen with the white lines.'

'I feel sick.' Stephanie turned her pale face away from the machine. 'I hate having a needle stuck in my hand.'

'It should be out tomorrow. You'll be back home before you know it. Then you can come over to my place. We'll have a movie night, watch some Sherlock Holmes and Agatha Christie.'

A lady in a white uniform appeared from behind the white curtain. 'Sorry, love, visiting hours are over.'

'No worries. Okay, I'll see ya soon, Steph. Be in touch.'

'Thanks, Em.'

The nurse turned to Stephanie. 'Got a magazine here. Would you like to take a look?'

'Yes, thanks.'

'Be right back.'

The thick white sheets rubbed against Stephanie's feet. She could not remember the last time she had been to hospital. The cool air from the air-conditioning blew on her face. The sound of footsteps echoed outside her door. Staring at the white curtain that surrounded her bed, she wondered if there was anyone else in her room. She had heard movement that she presumed had come from the other bed.

'Here you go,' the nurse had returned with the magazine. 'I'll be back soon.'

'Thank you.' Stephanie said with half a smile.

Flipping through the magazine pages she read a few of the headlines 'Lose weight in 20 days' and 'How to have a perfect relationship'. Too tired to read, she decided to look at the photos. One page displayed ladies standing on a red carpet. They looked so glamorous in their slinky dresses. Their tall figures stood proudly as they placed their hands on their hips. Smiling with their pearly white teeth, the models vibrant red lipstick projected off their pouted lips. Stephanie giggled. It was funny how a little bit of red would smudge onto Andrew's lips after they kissed.

Stephanie brushed a piece of hair that had fallen in front of her eyes. She sank back into the bed and allowed it to cushion her weary body. Her eyes noticed the models with their slim figures. Stephanie never felt she looked like a model but did not care as she had Andrew.

The paper crumpled as she turned the page. Stephanie stared at a gluten free chocolate cake. Just the sight of food made her feel sick.

Chapter Five

'Good morning, Stephanie. I'm Dr. Randle. I hope you're feeling a bit better today?'

'Morning already?'

'Yes, you must have slept well.'

'I don't remember. It's all a blur.'

Dr. Randle took a look at his notes. 'I spoke to your parents yesterday. They said you've never collapsed before?'

Stephanie nodded. 'Not that I can remember.'

'I see … ' Dr. Randle kept reading his notes. 'Anyway, you look a lot better and I've got some good news. As soon as the nurse has disconnected the heart monitor and taken the drip out, you can go home. But I want you to take it easy. Are you still at school or working?'

'After the summer holidays I'll be in Year 12. I have a summer job at the moment.'

Dr. Randle raised his eyebrows and stroked his chin. 'Year 12 is a big year. My son just went through that. How are you feeling about it?'

'I was excited … but since … Andrew … I'm not looking forward to it.'

'I see, your parents did mention – '

'Andrew was my boyfriend.'

'I'm very sorry to hear,' Dr. Randle said with a sense of sadness in his voice. 'Was he going into Year 12 too?'

'He'd finished school,' Stephanie said in a muffled voice.

'I see. Well, just take it easy. Don't push yourself too hard. I would like to see you in a couple of weeks, just to see how you're going. Any questions for me?'

'I don't think so. Thank you, Dr. Randle.'

'You're welcome, Stephanie. The nurse will be in soon.'

The other bed was empty now so Stephanie was alone. Hospital was a place she had rarely visited and for that she was thankful. Andrew's death had been so sudden and unexpected. Before that Stephanie had everything planned. Her summer job at the library and facing Year 12 but now nothing seemed to matter. Andrew was so important to her and now he was gone.

'Good morning, dear,' said the nurse as she entered the room. 'I'm just going to disconnect the heart monitor and take out the drip. Then you're free to go home.' Her voice was comforting. 'Do you have anything planned for the day?'

Stephanie shrugged her shoulders. 'I think I'll go straight home and rest.'

'Most people like to go straight home.'

There was an uncomfortable silence.

'Finished already?' Stephanie was shocked how quickly the nurse had attended to her needs. 'I didn't even feel you take the drip out. I was a bit worried. I hate needles.'

'Not many people are fans of needles but it's over now.'

'So now what?' Stephanie asked.

'I'll call your parents to come and get you. You can wait in the waiting room until they arrive.'

'Okay, thank you.'

Stephanie waited for her parents to come. She really did not like being in the hospital. A man was constantly sneezing and blowing his nose. She was very tempted to read a magazine just to pass the time but nothing took her interest. She missed Andrew and wondered how she could ever replace the hole in her heart. Another person walked into the waiting room. Now there were three people in the room. The girl started playing on her phone.

Stephanie reflected on what she used to do on weekends before she met Andrew. Dancing had played a major part in her life. She would go to a jazz class for an hour and loved the exercise. She sighed, Andrew had suggested she go back to dancing. Stephanie did not want to go back to jazz dancing, she wanted to try a new style of dance. Without thinking, she was on her mobile searching Google. She typed in the word 'dance'.

'Sexy Latin American Guru of Dance' appeared on the screen. *Latin American dancing, I have never done that before,* she thought as she hit the link. Squinting at the bright, red letters that appeared on the screen, she read the words – 'Lust and love, master the craft of dance at Dance Discovery - 400 Church Street, Richmond, Victoria.'

Her eyes darted back and forth across the screen. There was no information on days or times, just a contact number – 'Call Anton for further information on 9429 4666'. She scribbled the number down on a piece of paper that she found in her bag and thought she would call it later.

'Stephanie,' a familiar voice said.

'Mum, Dad, you're here. Thank goodness.'

The drive home was about fifteen minutes. Stephanie stared out the window as her father drove.

'Stephanie, you look a little pale.'

'I just need some fresh air, the hospital was so stuffy.' Her eyes focused on the outside world.

'Well, you're outta there now and we'll be home any minute,' her father said cheerfully as he turned up the radio.

'Time for our flashback song of the day. Here's "Perhaps" from *Strictly Ballroom* …'

Stephanie focused on the jumpy beat as she tapped her feet in time to the music.

'Mum … I think I want to learn Latin dancing.'

'Oooo! Latin dancing?'

'Yeah, I searched on my phone there's a dance school in Richmond called Dance Discovery.'

'When are the classes?'

'I'm not sure but there was a number. I'll call later and find out.' Stephanie started to cough.

'Oh love, are you okay?' her mother was worried.

Stephanie groaned. 'I just caught some cold air in my lungs. I'm fine.'

'Home soon. We'll drop you off and then get some groceries. You can go and rest.'

'Thanks Mum.'

As the Mazda 3 travelled along the road, the smell of fish and chips wafted in the air. A few people were making their way out of the bakery and along the shopping strip. Stephanie stared at the street sign as the car turned the corner.

'Should I walk in with you?'

'Nah, I'm fine,' she assured as she closed the car door and then waved to her parents. 'Back soon, love!'

Stephanie placed her bag on the floor, threw her mobile on the table and collapsed on the black leather couch. She flipped her shoes off her feet and wiggled her toes. The schoolbooks and sheets of notes were still piled on the table but it was the photo in the wooden frame that caught Stephanie's attention. The blue evening gown draped elegantly on her slim figure. Andrew's arms were wrapped around her waist. Dressed in a black suit, he looked proud with a smile on his face. She remembered dancing with him on that night. How magical the evening had been. She had worn her silver pair of high heels for the first time and felt like Cinderella. Nicole had not thought that was a good idea, you need to break them in, but she had been wrong and Stephanie had danced the night away. If Stephanie could capture a moment in time and hold it forever this would be the one.

Stephanie huffed as she thought back to her last conversation with Andrew. He had encouraged her to start dance classes again. She grabbed her mobile and searched for the number. Picking up the home phone, she punched in the number and waited.

'Thanks for calling Dance Discovery. If you are calling regarding class times, please press 1 – '

Stephanie hit 1.

'We offer two beginner group classes on Thursday and Friday nights at 7 p.m. Intermediate classes are held on – '

She hung up the receiver. *Thursday is tomorrow!* Stephanie's thoughts raced as she started to dream about what she should wear. It would not be like other dance classes. In ballet they wore a tutu and jazz, a leotard. *But what do Latin dancers wear?*

Stephanie could smell her favourite floral fragrance as she entered her room. Clothes were still scattered over the floor just how she had left them. Her wardrobe creaked as she opened the old wooden door. A black casual dress that came just above the knees was hanging within hands reach. Stephanie pulled it out and flung the dress onto the bed. *Hmm, sexy,* she thought.

'Steph, we're home! Are you hungry?'

Stephanie's thoughts were interrupted by her mother's voice. She made her way to the kitchen.

'How are you feeling?' her mother asked.

'Yeah, okay … '

Her mother placed the groceries on the bench and then gave Stephanie a hug.

'I know it's hard,' she whispered. 'Your dad and I are here to support you. We love you. I'll make us a hot chocolate and then we can have a chat. You go and sit on the couch.'

Stephanie stared at the black television screen.

'Don't want to turn it on?' Her mother asked.

'I'd rather not at the moment.' She was busy listening to the whistle of the kettle as the steam rose.

'Nearly ready, milk with one sugar.'

The cup was placed on the coffee table as Jane sat next to her daughter. 'Stephanie, I called Emma yesterday and she suggested I speak to Ally. After chatting to her she wants you to come back when you're feeling better.'

Stephanie sighed. 'I like working at the library but I need time. Thanks for calling her though.' She eyed the chocolate biscuits that lay on the coffee table.

'Go on, have one.' Her mother offered her the plate. 'I'm glad you're going back to dancing, you've always loved it. It's a shame you stopped.' Jane took a sip of her hot chocolate.

'I called the dance school while you were out.'

'When are the classes?'

'Thursday and Friday nights at seven, I was thinking of going tomorrow night.'

Her mother nodded. 'If you're feeling up to it, I think it's a great idea. Will you go by train?

'Yeah, I think so.'

'I would take you but the child care centre wants me to work late and your father won't get home till about six.'

'I'll be fine on the train.'

Biscuit crumbs fell onto Stephanie's plate as she took another bite into the delicious cookie. 'This tastes good.'

Jane smiled. 'I'll have to make some more. You need fattening up!'

Stephanie picked up another biscuit. 'I haven't felt like eating much recently but these cookies are so yummy. I love them.'

Jane put her arm around Stephanie. 'You're so sweet, gorgeous girl.' She kissed her on the cheek. 'Let's get some rest. I've got work tomorrow and you need to take it easy.'

She picked up the two plates and mugs and made her way into the kitchen.

'Thanks, Mum. I love you,' Stephanie called out to her mother.

The comforting voice of her mother had made her feel much better.

She changed into her pink pyjamas and climbed under the sheets. For the first time since Andrew's death, she did not feel alone. Stephanie rested her weary head on the soft pillow. Turning onto her side, she gently closed her eyes.

Chapter Six

The sunlight peeked through the crack in the curtain.

Stephanie opened her eyes. Sprawled across her mattress, she looked at her bedside clock. *Midday already!* she thought.

Wrapping her dressing gown around herself, she made her way into the kitchen. Shivering as her feet touched the cold tiled floor, she hurried over to the kettle. Steam rose from the kettle as the water finished boiling. The sweet aroma of coffee drifted in the air as it was tipped off the spoon and into the cup.

She could hear her mobile ringing. 'Mum' flashed up on the screen.

'Morning! Did you sleep well?'

'Yeah, I did,' she answered groggily.

'Oh sorry, love. Did I wake you up?'

'No, I'm just making myself a coffee.'

'I hope you're eating something as well?'

'Of course, Mum,' Stephanie groaned as she finished adding the milk into her cup.

'Anyway, just on my lunch break and ringing in to check up. Are you still thinking of going to the dance class tonight?'

'Yeah, I'd like to give it a try.'

'I think you should. I spoke to Emma and she said she would give you a call.'

Stephanie sat at the breakfast table and put her mum on loudspeaker.

'Cool, thanks.'

'Take care, darling.'

Stephanie hung up the phone. She breathed in the coffee smell as the steam rose from her cup. It was too hot to drink. She crossed her arms and waited. She could feel her bones sticking out. This was something she had never experienced before. She was about to take a sip of her drink when the doorbell rang.

Stephanie opened the door to see Emma's freckly face in front of her.

Emma stepped inside. 'I've come to pick you up!'

'Huh?' Stephanie raised her eyebrows.

'I don't mean to sound bossy but you have ten minutes to get out of your pyjamas and then I'm going to take you somewhere.' Her brown eyes stared at Stephanie.

'But, Em … ' Stephanie protested.

'No further questions, just get ready! I'll see you in the car.' Emma started making her way down the path.

'Should I put down the window?' Stephanie took a deep breath. The car was stuffy.

'Sure, go ahead.'

'Em, I need to tell you something. I've not said anything to my parents yet but – '

'What are you planning?' Emma was hesitant.

'It's nothing bad. I just don't think they'll be happy about it.'

'That doesn't sound good. I'm worried.'

'Don't be. It's just … I just don't want to go back to school this year.' Stephanie took a bite of her fingernail. 'It's my final year but I know I won't be able to cope. I've always got good grades but – '

'But what?' Emma was concerned.

'Andrew was around then. Everything is different now.'

'Stephanie, that's a big decision to make.'

'I'll probably go back next year but at the moment I know I'll struggle to get good grades. It's just a lot of pressure that I don't need right now.'

Emma continued to concentrate on her driving. 'I'm not sure what to advise but I guess people take gap years. Usually after they finish school they may decide to travel. A lot of my friends have actually, Katy went to England and never came back.'

'A gap year that's what I want, this year I was thinking I could work at the library.'

Emma gave her a glance. 'Ally's always looking for an extra pair of hands. I think she would agree to that.'

'But now I have to convince my parents,' Stephanie groaned.

'Just be truthful. Tell them what you told me.'

'I guess. Anyway, where are we going?' Stephanie bit another fingernail.

'Okay, so the other week I was walking past a crystal shop and saw they had a sign saying "crystal ball readings" – '

'Is that safe?' Stephanie interrupted. She touched a lump that was starting to form in her throat.

'I have a friend who had her cards read, I guess this would be similar but with a crystal ball. What do you have to lose? I think you should give it a try.' Emma did not seem concerned.

'I'll give it a go but I don't know what my parents will think.'

'I would never let you do anything that was dangerous. You just want some answers, don't you?'

'I guess so,' Stephanie looked back at Emma.

'Great, so that's where we are going, the crystal shop,' Emma smiled widely.

Stephanie stared out the window. 'I've never done anything like this before.'

'You'll be fine. Trust me. I'm like your big sister.'

'Nicole said her family would never allow her in a crystal shop.'

'Nicole who?'

'My friend from school.'

Emma rolled her eyes. 'Some people have weird ideas.'

'Nicole's family is very religious, a strict orthodox family.'

'That explains it. Just give it a try. Who knows what you may find out.'

Stephanie bit off another nail.

'I've made an appointment for you.'

'Really?' Stephanie was surprised.

'Yep, I planned it all. I'll drop you out the front, find a spot and wait in the shop till you've finished. I think they've got a little café area. And by the way, we don't have to tell anyone about this. It can be our secret.'

Stephanie turned to face Emma. 'I don't think we should tell anyone.'

'Yeah, we won't. Look, a parking spot right out the front of the shop. It must be our lucky day! I've just got to make a phone call then I'll be coming in. Don't wait for me. Good luck!'

'Thanks, Em.'

Chapter Seven

Stephanie could hear the tinkling of chimes as they blew in the breeze.

She had walked past many crystal shops before but had never been inside. Her hand pushed aside the dangling door decorations that covered the entrance. The sweet musky smell of burning incense wafted around the room. Magnificent coloured crystals were on show in cabinets. Placed on shelves were statues of angels and other figures. Sparkling necklaces, bangles and other jewellery caught her eye. On the wall signs displayed words saying imagine, believe and destiny.

'Can I help you?'

'Hi, I'm Stephanie. My friend Emma made an appointment for me?'

'Oh yes, you've been booked in for the crystal ball session with Madam Farrell. She shouldn't be too long. Please feel free to take a look around.'

'Thank you.'

A pale pink crystal caught Stephanie's eye. Rose quartz the label read, the crystal of unconditional love. She wanted to touch the crystal. As she continued to browse, Stephanie could hear the shop assistant chatting to a customer at the front counter.

'You ordered an incense burner and emeralds. I don't think they have arrived yet. '

'Really! I've been waiting for ages. Where is Ana? I usually deal with her.'

'I think she's out the back, I'll check.'

The man tapped his fingers on the counter as he waited impatiently.

'Sorry Bruno, I rang them last week and they told me they had sent them.'

A girl with long dark hair stood at the counter.

'Ana, it's taking too long. I trusted you with my order.'

'Sorry, there's not much else I can do ... '

'I guess I'll have to wait,' he huffed under his breath.

'Voy a tu casa esta noche,' she whispered in a foreign language. He nodded and left the shop.

Stephanie wondered what language the girl had spoken in. *Perhaps Italian? Or maybe it was Spanish?*

'Ah, rose quartz - the love crystal. You should get one,' the shop assistant said as she walked over to Stephanie.

'I don't know much about crystals,' Stephanie admitted.

'I learnt about them in my country.'

'Where are you from?'

'I was born in South America.'

'South America I've never been there.'

'I came to Australia with my family when I was fifteen.'

'Do you like it here?'

'It's okay. I'll go back there one day but I think my parents will stay here now. They've made some good friends. Actually, they know the man who I just spoke to.'

'Really.'

'Latinos stick together. Not saying that in a rude way. But it's hard when you first come here and don't speak the language.'

Something soft rubbed against Stephanie's leg.

Meowwww …

'I can see you have just met Midnight,' said a voice.

Stephanie looked up to find a lady with sparkling green eyes standing in front of her.

'I'll leave you to it.' The Latino girl walked away.

'Hello, I'm Madam Farrell. Are you Stephanie?'

'Yes.'

The lady held out her hand. 'Lovely to meet you. Follow me.'

'Enjoy your session.' The girl mumbled.

They made their way up a winding staircase. Chimes hung from the ceiling. A Buddha and an angel statue were placed at the top of the stairs.

'Not many people have crystal balls these days.' Madam Farrell turned to Stephanie. 'They are becoming a thing of the past. People are using Tarot cards.' She guided Stephanie into a small room. 'Please take a seat.'

A large round crystal ball rested on a red crushed velvet cloth that was draped on a table in the middle of the room. The sound of waves crashing played in the background. Candlelight lit the room. Madam Farrell sat on the other side of the crystal ball, her green eyes gazing into Stephanie's. As she leaned forward her dark curly locks hung past her shoulders. She covered her hair with her dark purple hood, the candlelight lighting up her pale face.

'Now, Stephanie, the way I like to do this is for you to shut your eyes and relax while I focus on the crystal ball and your future.'

Stephanie closed her eyes and took a deep breath.

'I know why you're here. You want answers.' Madam Farrell commenced.

'Nothing makes sense,' Stephanie replied. 'I can't understand why it happened to me.'

'There's a reason you are sitting in this chair, you've been brought to me.'

'Really?'

'Please, I need silence for a minute. I see a man with dark hair in my crystal ball. Do you know who he is?'

'It could be Andrew?'

'Yes, I'm getting an A with this image. Mmm … Andrew … not sure if it's an Andrew – '

'Andrew's dead,' Stephanie interrupted harshly. She could feel her eyes watering but kept them shut.

'This man is alive. He could already be in your life or is about to enter soon. He's tall and attractive and many females are drawn to him.'

Stephanie was confused. She could not think of anyone who fitted that description, except Andrew.

'This man is going to have a big influence on you. He'll help you connect with your true self. You have lost that recently. Is that true?'

'I've not really felt myself.'

'Wait a minute, I see something else, this image is not clear. I'm getting another male presence with a connection to the letter B. This is not good energy, so beware. The only other connection I can see is the A and B men are linked in some way. Is there someone in your life starting with a B?'

'No.'

'Interesting, the image is fading and a new scene has appeared?'

'What's the scene?'

'A beach.' Madam Farrell suddenly stopped talking.

Stephanie wanted to open her eyes but she resisted as the silence was making her feel uncomfortable. She swallowed and waited for more.

'I can see you have a strong connection with the sun, Stephanie.'

'I do like the beach but I've never really thought about my connection with the sun.' Stephanie was confused.

'Now I know why I was guided to play the beach music in your session. Something has happened to you at the beach and more than once.'

Stephanie clenched her fist. *How does this lady know so much?* she thought. *Remain calm. Try to relax. Breathe in, breathe out.* Stephanie focused on her breath. She allowed her chest to rise and fall.

'Deep breaths, in and out. Do not allow your thoughts to take over. Stay in the present. Animals, I see some animals.' Madam Farrell's voice was rushed, 'A bird, a cat and a snake. Interesting … Do you have a pet bird or cat?'

'No, no pets.'

'Let me rephrase the question. Have you ever had a pet?'

'No, but I always wanted one.'

'Maybe these images of animals are symbolic then.'

'In what way?'

'I like the image of the bird and cat but I'm not too sure about the snake. We don't have enough time to go into all this today, but I can tell you there are a lot of interesting happenings ahead of you. My advice to you is you need to stay strong. I know you are a strong woman. Things are not going to get better nor are they going to get worse. Trust your gut and go with what you feel. The images have all gone now, meaning the crystal ball does not want to reveal anymore. Please take a moment to reflect and gently open your eyes when you're ready.'

The lighted candle was the first object Stephanie saw when she opened her eyes. Madam Farrell had taken off her hood now and was sitting patiently waiting for Stephanie.

'I feel you're not sleeping well. Is that correct?'

'I just can't seem to switch off my thoughts.'

'I want you to buy a rose quartz crystal and some lavender oil. Put the rose quartz crystal under your pillow at night and during the day carry the crystal in your bag. At night put two drops of lavender on your pillow. Crystals have healing powers. I think that's what we'll start with.'

'I don't know a lot about crystals.'

'Follow me.'

Madam Farrell and Stephanie made their way back down the staircase and into the shop. It looked a lot brighter than when she was there before.

'Here they are, the beautiful rose quartz.'

Stephanie could not believe her eyes. That was the crystal she had been drawn to when she first entered the shop.

'How do I know which one to choose?'

'Go with how you feel.'

Stephanie reached out her hand and picked up a smooth pale pink crystal. She placed it gently in the middle of her palm. 'This one feels right.'

'So take it. Before you leave I'll show you the small bottles of lavender oil. This will encourage restful sleep. You look tired.'

'I am a little.'

'It has been lovely to meet you, dear. You can pay for your items at the counter. Remember follow your instincts. If you know it's wrong, then you are probably right.' Madam Farrell turned around and walked back towards the stairs, her long purple robe swishing around her body.

Stephanie was speechless when she placed her items on the counter.

'Can I help you with anything else?'

'I also need to pay for my crystal ball session.'

'That's been paid for, just the rose quartz $5 and lavender oil $3, a total of $8 for today.'

'Thank you.' Stephanie handed over the money.

'Would you like to book a follow up reading?'

'Not at this stage.'

'Well, you know where we are and can always call. Have a great day. Hope to see you again.'

Stephanie walked into the café area where Emma was patiently waiting. Her phone and car keys rested on the table.

'How did it go?'

'I'm not really sure. Maybe I need time to reflect. But thanks for paying for the session.'

Emma grinned. 'No worries, I hope it helped in some way. Let's drop you home.'

As they walked to the car, Stephanie still had so many unanswered questions in her mind. *Why had a bird, cat and snake appeared in the crystal ball? What did they symbolise?* Her other question was still unanswered – why had this happened to her?

Emma had not asked her many questions in the car. She was relieved about that – but more importantly, tonight was the dance class.

Stephanie was glad to return home and was excited to be putting on her silky dress. It actually felt quite loose. It had been a long time since she had worn it.

Admiring her reflection in the mirror, Stephanie brushed her long brown hair and put it into a ponytail securing it with a hair clip. She applied some black mascara that made her long eyelashes stand out. Next was the rich berry lipstick that covered her soft lips. She was ready, she felt sexy.

Stephanie dragged herself away from the mirror and put on a jacket. She snatched her bag and headed for the door.

Chapter Eight

Stephanie stood on the platform and waited.

The bright orange line along the edge of the platform separated the passengers from the train. This warned travellers of the potential danger they may face. Men in business suits stood waiting to head home from work. She had caught the train to Richmond many times to watch the football at the Melbourne Cricket Ground. Andrew's football team was the Melbourne Demons and he had convinced her to barrack for them too. Together they had watched the boys wearing the red and blue. Stephanie had liked the fact that the colours were red and blue but she disliked that their mascot was a demon. The word demon made her think of evil.

This was the first time she had caught the train to Richmond alone. Single again, she felt isolated from the world. Couples seemed to be everywhere. A young couple stood metres away from her, the guy had his arms wrapped around his girlfriend's waist. She was giggling as he whispered into her ear. An elderly couple stood holding hands as they waited for the train. Stephanie sighed. She missed Andrew, listening to his words and holding his hand. Andrew used to put his arm around her when they waited for the train on their way to the football. Stephanie could see the train arriving. The rattling noise amplified as it drew nearer. A few faces peered out the windows.

Choosing a vacant seat, she placed her bag underneath as the sliding door closed. The seat next to her was empty. She longed for Andrew to be sitting there. She could almost visualise him, holding her hand and whispering in her ear. *I miss his company,* she thought. *I miss the sound of his voice. The world seems to have become a scarier place. I felt safer when Andrew was around. Now here I am travelling alone.*

A bald guy across the carriage with muscular arms suddenly sneezed. Stephanie looked over at him. Red, blue and black covered his arms. Stephanie had never liked tattoos. His beady eyes stared over at her.

Please don't come and sit next to me, she thought as she looked out the window, trying to avoid eye contact. Just then, the train stopped at South Yarra Station. *Next stop, Richmond. What a relief!*

As she stepped onto the platform, the bitter wind blew her hair around her face. The sky was grey and uninviting. Stephanie shivered as the cold night air seeped through her jacket and onto her back. She tucked her hands into her jacket pockets.

Where is this dance school? she thought to herself as she walked down the steps from the platform.

The long street lay ahead of her. She walked past a pub, a Mexican restaurant and a crystal shop. Passing the traffic lights at the intersection, she turned into Church Street. The street was empty, not a person in sight. Her eyes were then drawn to a bright yellow sign reading 'Dance Discovery'. She had arrived.

Her hands trembled as she opened the front door. There was soft rhythmic music playing in the background as she made her way up the stairs. Stephanie could hear a loud voice with a strong accent.

'Now, you've made sure you separated the cash from the other stuff? It must be in a different place.'

Stephanie approached the front desk. A girl with dark hair and an olive complexion was sitting behind it. A tall Latino man with short brown hair and tan skin had his hand on her shoulder.

'Make sure you get it right.'

'Yes, Bruno.'

Frowning at Stephanie, he walked away.

'Sorry about that. I'm Becky.'

'I'm Stephanie.'

'Welcome! Are you here for the beginner's dance class?'

'Yeah, I've never done Latin dancing before.'

'That's okay, the beginner class goes over the steps,' Becky smiled.

Stephanie sighed. 'How much is the class?'

'Twenty dollars.'

Stephanie rummaged around in her bag, searching for her purse. She pulled out an orange note and placed it into the girl's hand.

'Thank you, I hope you enjoy the class. If you just want to wait over there with the others, the class will start in about ten minutes.'

The dance studio had polished wooden floorboards and white walls. Posters covered the walls showing dancers in various poses. A floor to ceiling mirror was positioned along the length of one side of the dim room and a disco ball hung from the ceiling.

Stephanie decided to sit down and wait for the class to begin. As her eyes circled the room, she noticed most of the other students were female. A sense of fear overcame Stephanie. *Will I cope with the dance steps?* she wondered.

Her mind wandered back to an occasion when she was seven. She had been dressed in a pink tutu for a school concert. On the stage she had danced for the audience and enjoyed every minute but the girl next to her had made a mistake and burst into tears. The whole performance was stopped and everyone rushed off the stage. Stephanie had felt so sorry for her.

The world of Latin dancing was unfamiliar to Stephanie. In the ballet studio there were bars for the ballerinas to hold and practice their arabesques. Before jazz classes the dancers would be warming up doing their stretches on the floor. When class began they would move around the studio in their aerobic gear and some even chose to wear sweatbands and leggings. But these girls were different. They wore black high-heeled dance shoes and sexy black and red, short dresses. Many had chosen to wear makeup. It looked like they were ready to have a night out on the town instead of getting hot and sweaty.

Stephanie looked at her watch. *Five minutes to go,* she thought as she bit her nail. A tall, muscular man with shoulder length, dark curly hair and tan skin caught her eye. He was wearing black pants and a tight fitting top. He walked over. Stephanie took a deep breath as his eyes met hers.

'Hi, are you here to do the beginner dance class?'

'Yeah, I am.' Stephanie nodded.

He folded his muscular arms. 'I'm Anton, the dance teacher. Have you danced before?'

'When I was younger, but never Latin dancing.'

'Sorry, I didn't get your name?' Anton's eyes gazed into Stephanie's as he waited for her response.

'Stephanie,' she replied, feeling a little awkward.

His gaze became more intense. 'Welcome, Stephanie. I hope you enjoy the class.'

'Thank you,' she said as she felt her face starting to flush. Why was she feeling like this?

'I'll be right back and we'll get started,' Anton said before disappearing into the back room.

The steady beat of the music soon filled the dance studio. The other students made their way onto the dance floor.

Anton reappeared and positioned himself on the dance floor in front of the group facing the mirror. Preening himself like a peacock, he ran his fingers through his hair. Stephanie made her way towards the back of the group of students and when she turned around, Anton was staring at her.

'In tonight's class we'll be learning the Salsa.' A smirk appeared on his face. 'Watch as I demonstrate.'

His toned body moved as he swayed his hips. All the women seemed to be mesmerised by Anton's movements. They could not take their eyes off him.

'Look at his sexy butt … '

'Oh my god … '

Stephanie couldn't help but overhear the other girls whispering.

'Now, you try copying me,' suggested Anton, a cheeky grin sweeping across his face.

Stephanie took a deep breath and attempted the dance moves. She listened to the beat of the music and her feet started to move in time. Once again something in her life felt in sync. She started to lose herself in the music and her thoughts concentrated only on her dance steps. Her hips swayed as her eyes focused on the mirror image of herself.

'I think you're all starting to get the basic step of Salsa. I need ladies on one side of the room and men on the other side.'

Anton had interrupted the moment.

Stephanie quickly took her place next to the other females.

Anton walked into the centre of the room. 'Tam, come here please.'

A skinny Asian girl with long hair walked over to him.

'I need you to help me demonstrate the steps. The man always leads. You must wait until he starts to dance.'

Tam tried desperately to stare into Anton's eyes as they danced, but Anton seemed to avoid her eye contact completely. The movements were compact as they danced around the floor. Stephanie watched them move. The thought of dancing with a partner for the first time worried her. What would happen if she got a step wrong and clumsily trod on his foot? How embarrassed would she feel!

'When you start to dance with your partner it's important to feel the connection. The connection is the way to communicate.' Anton twirled around to face the women and smiled.

Stephanie sighed, she was confused and hoped this did not show on her face.

'I guess it's hard to explain you have to experience it to understand. It's about the dance movements between the lead and follow. In this case, Tam is the follower and moves to match my lead. I'll go into that more another night.'

Stephanie started to breathe deeply as she wondered if she would get to dance with Anton. *Who will be the next lucky girl?* she wondered.

'Right, this is how it works when you have chosen your partner. You dance with them for a while till I tell you to move to the next person on your right. We will be moving in a big circle anti-clockwise.'

Stephanie did not know what she thought about this. Maybe it was a way to get to know all the males in the class.

'Now, choose your partner,' Anton looked in Stephanie's direction.

Stephanie gasped as her eyes met the ground. The last time she remembered dancing was with Andrew at the high school formal – giggling and gazing into each other's eyes on the dance floor. She remembered his words.

'I'll never let you out of my arms, Stephanie …'

She had brushed his black hair behind his ear and wished the night would never end.

'I love you, Steph. I always will … '

Now it was all over and he was gone. She had to build a new life and live in the here and now.

Looking across the room she noticed the three males standing waiting to dance. The girl next to her started to giggle. No one had paired up, all the girls seemed hesitant to choose a partner.

'Go on, don't be shy,' Anton encouraged. 'We have ten in the class tonight, four boys and six girls, that includes Tam and I. So two girls will get to have a rest break in between.'

'There are always more girls,' hissed a tall girl with long hair.

'Yes, Melissa. I know.'

Two of the girls made their way across the room and introduced themselves to their partners. Three others still stood next to Stephanie, this included Tam.

'Stephanie, you can go and dance with Jacob.' Anton grabbed her hand and guided her over to a middle-aged man with greying hair.

'I'm Jacob, pleased to meet you.'

'I'm Stephanie.'

Anton continued to organise the other students until everyone had their positions and he was ready to begin.

'Right, I will start dancing with Tam. Everybody watch us first and then follow along. We will do the same steps as before and just keep repeating.'

The dance students watched Anton and Tam dance.

'Now it's your turn to follow along and to mirror the movements,' Anton said.

Stephanie danced with Jacob. She could not remember touching a man's hand since Andrew died. Holding Jacob's hands felt strange yet comforting. His hands were not like Andrew's – they were rough from age. Stephanie had forgotten what it was like to touch. Her whole body felt overwhelmed with emotions, sadness and happiness. *What am I doing here?* she asked herself.

'Change partners!' Anton turned again, facing Stephanie.

This time, he grabbed her hands and did not let go.

'Now we have our new partners. This time I want you to play around with the basic movements of Salsa that I've taught you. Doing this is called "freestyling".'

Stephanie smiled shyly this was the first time she was going to dance with Anton. Her hand trembled a little as she held his. *What if I make a mistake with one of the steps?* She could smell his musky aftershave as he matched her frame.

'You'll be fine, Steph. Just let me take the lead and you follow along.' He grinned at her.

Anton began to move and Stephanie followed hoping she would not step on his feet. His twinkling eyes stared down onto her. Or were his eyes sweeping up and down her body? Stephanie did not know where to look. Anton leaned in closer and before she knew it their bodies were touching. Stephanie liked the sensation of his body against hers.

'Change partners,' Anton told the students still holding her hand with a tight grip.

His eyes swept around the room making sure everyone had a new dance partner.

'Keep playing around with the steps. Off you go,' he added.

Stephanie caught Anton's gaze.

'Move those hips,' he whispered. 'Salsa is a sexy dance.'

A grin swept across his face. Stephanie wanted to smile but she held back. Moving her hips in this way felt awkward and unnatural. She had never danced like this before.

'Relax, Stephanie. Focus more on the feeling rather than the thinking. Let the movement become natural for you.'

'I'll try to.' She nodded.

At that moment Stephanie allowed herself to forget her worries. Her feet moved to the music. His muscular frame supported her.

'I can see you're enjoying yourself,' he whispered into her ear.

'I love to dance.'

'You must do it more.'

She did not know what to say. Anton was so charming and she wanted to keep dancing with him for as long as possible. The studio lights captured the disco ball allowing silver specks to cover the ceiling. Stephanie felt she had stepped into a dance movie and was playing one of the lead parts.

Anton unexpectedly turned her to face the mirror. She gasped and he smiled in response, knowing he had surprised her and was proud of his effort.

'Stay focused,' he said.

Stephanie continued to dance and follow his lead.

Latin dancing requires a partner, she thought. One is not possible without the other. You need to trust your partner. Hmmm …

The music suddenly stopped, interrupting her thoughts.

'I hope you all enjoyed the class tonight. All good things must come to an end.' Anton said as he let go of Stephanie's hands. 'Make sure you practice the steps before the next class. See you next time.' He left the dance floor and disappeared into the back room.

'Lovely dancing with you tonight,' Jacob said as he walked past Stephanie. 'See you at the next class.'

'Bye.'

Stephanie went to collect her bag. Walking past some other girls she overheard their conversation.

'Anton didn't dance with me tonight.'

'He only danced with Tam and that other new girl.' The two girls' eyes glared at Stephanie as she walked past.

'I wonder why he danced with her? Look at what she's wearing. No fashion sense at all. Let's wait till he comes out again. Maybe he'll come with us for a drink.' The girls continued chatting as Stephanie headed towards the stairs and made her way out into the cold night air.

Chapter Nine

'You're back! How was the dance class?' her mother called from the lounge room.

Stephanie's legs ached as she took off her shoes and rested on the couch. 'I'm a bit sore. I guess I'm not used to it.'

'What dance did you learn?'

'We learnt the Salsa. Just the basic steps, no routine.'

'That sounds like fun – '

'When you're dancing the Salsa you need to keep a close hold and a lot of the movement is in the lower body. I found it kinda difficult, but fun,' Stephanie interrupted.

'A lot of hip movement then?'

'Yeah, heaps. The lower half of the body is used a lot. But ...' she hesitated, 'well ... the difficult part wasn't actually the dancing ... '

Her mother turned down the volume as she looked at Stephanie. 'What was it then? Dancing with a partner?'

'Yeah ... I've only ever danced with Andrew before.'

'Oh Stephanie, it's good to learn to dance with others. Your dad can't dance to save himself, two left feet! It will feel more natural the more you do it.'

'Latin American dancing is very different to what I'm used to.

In jazz, it's not partner work you dance as a group and you're free to move.'

'It's very different.' Her mother agreed.

'I was told during the class that the man leads the movements. I'll get used to it. I did enjoy going.'

Stephanie rested her head on the back of the couch.

'Mum, I have to talk to you about something else. I'm not sure what you're going to think … '

'Oh, what's that?' her mother said, wanting to give her full attention.

Stephanie sighed. 'I don't want to do Year 12 this year … I just … I need to take time off. I've been thinking about this a lot – '

Her mother could not believe what she was hearing.

'Wait a minute, Steph – '

'I'll work in the library this year and – '

'I'm not sure this is the right idea.'

'Mum,' Stephanie pleaded. 'Since Andrew's death, I just can't focus. Year 12 is such a big year and I'm afraid I can't cope with it now.'

Her mother frowned. 'Mmm, this certainly isn't an easy decision.'

'Please,' Stephanie begged. 'I know it's not an easy decision but I would just be taking a break. People do it when they finish school. They travel.'

'That's different, Stephanie. They've finished school.'

Jane shook her head and Stephanie closed her eyes. This conversation was not going too well.

'Mum, I just don't feel I can cope with the pressure this year. Everything is different now Andrew's not here.'

'But your dad and I will support you,' her mother said.

'I know you will but I can't. Please understand. I'll probably go back next year but at the moment I know I won't be able to get good grades. It's just a lot of pressure that I don't need right now.'

'I don't want you to feel under pressure,' her mother whispered. 'I know you have had to deal with a lot recently, love. Here, give me a hug…'

Stephanie sighed. She hated having disagreements with her mother but in her heart this was something she knew she had to do. She could not go back to school, not now.

'I'll chat to your father. I feel you should keep working at the library. You need to be doing something constructive with your time.'

'I agree, Mum. Should I contact Ally?'

'Why don't we both go and have a chat with her. Would that be okay with you?'

'Would you mind if I work it out?' Stephanie muttered. She was hoping her father was not overhearing this discussion. 'I want to take responsibility for my decision.'

'Fair enough.'

Stephanie bit her nail, she could not believe her mother was starting to warm to the idea.

'You look tired darling. Why don't you go and rest.'

'I think I might. Goodnight, Mum.'

'Sweet dreams.'

Stephanie threw her clothes onto the bedroom floor and changed into her pyjamas. Her head lay on the soft pillow. She was out like a light.

Beep, beep, beep!

'Damn alarm clock, I hate the mornings,' she muttered

as she switched off the alarm and shut her eyes again. 'Five more minutes … no get up!' She groaned and ripped off the bedclothes. Removing her pyjamas and grabbing her pale blue shirt, she buttoned it up and put on her grey skirt.

Rushing into the kitchen, she noticed her mother had made a coffee. Stephanie reached for the mug and had a quick sip.

'Bye, Mum! Bye, Dad! I'm running late!' Grabbing her grey business jacket, she headed for the door.

People pushed and shoved as they made their way down the stairs and onto the platform at the train station. Stephanie looked at her watch. If she hadn't had that coffee she would have saved herself five minutes.

Stephanie watched the passing scene as the train travelled to her destination, with minutes to spare, she was making her way down Hampton Street. A mother with three children dressed in school uniform, was looking at her watch and telling them to hurry up and get into the car. Stephanie gasped it was her school's uniform.

As she continued walking she wondered if Nicole and Lizzy had been put in the same class and if Nicole had gone to any parties yet. She had not heard any gossip in ages - not one phone call from Nicole. School was becoming a distance memory as the days passed by.

Approaching the brick building she noticed in the front window of the library a sign announcing the community book fair coming soon. Stephanie huffed. *Great, another job I need to do,* she thought.

'I'm exhausted already,' she said as she flopped into the chair at the front desk.

Emma did not turn around she was busy typing on the computer. 'I got here before eight this morning.' Her eyes focused on the screen. 'I have so much to do.'

'So girls, what are your plans for the weekend?' Ally said as she entered the room. Her long, dark auburn hair was tied neatly in a ponytail so it would not fall onto her face. Emma stopped typing and turned around.

'I'll most likely be on Flirtnow all weekend. I've been chatting to this cool drummer guy.'

'Flirtnow?' Ally raised her eyebrows.

'It's a mobile dating app.'

'Dating app… mmm…not sure about that.' She fiddled with the clip in her hair. 'Anyway, I'm going on a third date with Shane. He's so much better than the last guy Adam, who only lasted three weeks.' She smiled widely. 'Last weekend Shane took me to that pub in Sandringham. We had a lovely view overlooking the beach. I'm hoping next time he'll take me for a fine dining experience.' She shook her head. 'Men today, do they really know what women want?'

Stephanie looked at Emma, had Ally become the new expert on dating?

'Anyway, are you feeling better?'

'Much better, thanks.' Stephanie took a deep breath.

'Glad to hear, we love having an extra pair of hands at the library.'

Stephanie sighed. 'Work keeps me busy. I love working here. So many interesting people to meet.' She sunk into her chair as Ally walked past.

'Glad she's gone,' Emma hissed. 'She was starting to give me a headache.'

Stephanie smiled and excused herself from the counter making her way to the bathroom. A tear rolled down her cheek as memories of Andrew re-entered her head.

She ran her hands under the cold water and splashed her face. The noise of the hand dryer rang in her ears. *Damn Ally and Emma, they don't really understand true love,* she thought. Ally seemed to have a different boyfriend all the time and it seemed like Emma had never had a serious relationship. It was different chatting to them compared to Nicole. She wondered if Nicole had spoken to Jim yet. She knew how badly she wanted a boyfriend.

Stephanie sighed. *No one will ever be like Andrew,* she thought. She missed him so much but had to block out her thoughts and focus on work. Fridays at the library were full of constant book organising, data entry and re-shelving the books. Before leaving the bathroom she looked at her reflection in the mirror for what seemed like the hundredth time. She only noticed now that her mascara was smudged. Ripping off a piece of paper towel, she dabbed her eyes and returned to her desk.

The library seemed to be a lot quieter.

'Can I please return this book?' A lady placed a large black book with golden writing on the front counter. 'I found this book fascinating. The Incas were an interesting race of people. I really want to visit South America one day. I have visited Egypt and seen the pyramids but South America is on my list now.'

Stephanie looked at the book. The gold title contrasted beautifully with the dark background of the cover – *The Undiscovered Worlds of Peru.*

'The Inca civilization had a wealth of gold. I learnt that gold was related to the sun and silver to the moon,' the lady's eyes twinkled as she spoke. 'There was so much symbolism in their world. I read the book in less than a week.'

'I may have to borrow this,' Stephanie muttered.

'Yes, you should. Better be on my way. Thanks, dear.'

Symbolism – that word had come up in Madam Farrell's conversation with Stephanie. She picked up a pile of books and dumped them on top.

Carrying the books, she made her way to the Non-Fiction section of the library. One by one, she placed the books back onto the shelves.

'Excuse me, you could help me?' A young girl with long blonde hair had approached Stephanie. 'Are you the librarian?'

'No, but I do work here. How can I help you?'

'I was wondering if you have any books on crystals or gemstones?'

'Are you looking for a particular crystal or gemstone?'

'No, I just want to read general information about them.'

'I'll take you to the area where the books should be. If there's not any suitable book there, you can do a catalogue search.'

'Thank you.'

Stephanie pointed to a shelf. 'This would be the place but there doesn't seem to be a lot. Here's one that says "gemstones".'

The girl observed the cover. 'Thanks, I'll start with that one.'

'Mum, I want a book about space.' A little boy said as she strolled along the aisle.

Stephanie loved working in the library and watching people of all ages reading. Reading had always been part of her life. Her first visit to the library had been with her grandma when she was in the first grade of school. Together they had got her a library card and borrowed a picture book. From that day on, Stephanie had wanted to keep returning to the library and reading books became a passion.

Returning the books to the shelves was her next task, there were only three books left. The first two books were easy as they were both in the same section. Now there was only one. Her eyes stared at the golden writing.

'*The Undiscovered Worlds of Peru* ...' Stephanie mumbled under her breath. She flicked through a few of the timeworn pages as her mind began to wonder. One particular page took her interest. She read the words carefully:

Peru is a country on the eastern side of the Pacific rim. The Peruvian civilization included the natural world in their artworks. Dynamic depictions of animals and birds decorated their art.

Stephanie quivered. Madam Farrell had seen animals in the crystal ball and had wondered if these animals were symbolic. Flipping through some more pages, she convinced herself that she must read this book. Taking it back to the front counter, Stephanie borrowed the book and placed it in her bag.

Chapter Ten

Stephanie sighed as she left the library – it had been a long day.

The afternoon air was crisp as she hurried to the station. People were scattered all over the platform. A man bumped into Stephanie as he walked past.

'Excuse me,' he said as he continued on.

'Get past her,' she heard someone else mutter.

She could hear the train approaching. As it stopped people rushed through the sliding doors. There were no vacant seats. Stephanie made her way to a less crowded area. Her hand reached for the pole to support her lanky body as she stared out the window. The scent of cigarettes wafted under her nose as a man in a brown trench coat sat below her. His enormous hands rested in his lap. Her left shoulder felt heavy as the strap of her bag pushed into her skin. It was the weight from the book she had borrowed. She wished she could pull it out and read but there really was way too many distractions to focus on the words.

Many schoolgirls occupied the carriage - some had piercings, others chewed gum. This reminded Stephanie of her journeys on the bus. She turned and listened in on the conversation of two girls who stood next to her. They were around the same age as her.

'Do you think he likes me?'

'Well, he hasn't called you for a week.'

'Maybe he's been busy. Do you think I should call him?'

'Mmm … maybe leave it another week.'

Stephanie wondered what her school friends were doing. She hadn't seen them all summer holidays. The girl chatting looked a lot like Jan. And the conversation about boys reminded her of Nicole.

'Ughhh, I just want to know if he likes me!'

The two girls were still debating what they should do.

'I know Jessica likes him too,' one said.

'Look, give it a few more days,' suggested the other.

Stephanie sighed remembering the days when she used to give Jeanette advice when she was dating Andrew. Jeanette had spent a lot of her time being single as her parents were not too keen on her dating.

As the train came to a stop, the two girls made their way out the door. They seemed to be heading in the same direction. Turning into the side street, Stephanie breathed a sigh of relief. *Nearly there*, she thought.

'Is anyone home?' Steph called out. She could hear the hum of the fridge as she walked past the kitchen and headed for the bathroom.

Placing her clothes over the silver towel rail, she opened the shower door and turned on the taps. As she stepped in, the warm water soothed her aching back. It was the first time all day that she had felt relaxed. The fresh, sweet smell of lavender drifted in the air around her as she lathered the soap over her body. She watched the condensation dripping down the glass door. Sitting on the shower floor, she relaxed. Her weary body leaned against the cool glass panel. The hot water trickled in her mouth and over her naked body, as she closed her eyes. She breathed gently and let the steam gather inside her lungs. Her foggy thoughts were clearing and her tears subsided.

The word 'dance' crept into her mind and a vision of her dancing with Anton emerged. She remembered his gaze and how their bodies swayed to the music. The water continued to drizzle over her lips and into her mouth. It trickled down the inside of her throat. She continued to get lost in her thoughts. Holding his hands and moving to the beat – she'd wanted him to kiss her.

Opening her eyes, she stared at a tiny drop of water that was making its way down the door. Taking a deep breath the drop reminded her of the day she walked along the pier. How close she had come to ending her life.

STOP! she thought.

Stephanie switched off the taps and grabbed the chestnut towel from the floor and wrapped it around her wet body. Her phone began to ring. It was Emma. *Perfect timing*, she thought. Her wet hair flicked around her face.

'Hey Em. What's up?'

'I'm fine. Just calling to remind you about the dating app, Flirtnow. One word, not two. Got that?' Emma asked.

'Yeah, thanks.'

'And the picture is of Cupid with a bow and arrow shooting at a heart. I'm talking to that drummer guy, Oliver.'

'Okay cool, I'll check it out.'

'It's fun and gives you something else to think about.'

Stephanie yawned as Emma kept chatting.

'Well I better go, Steph. Oliver awaits!

'Okay. Thanks Em. Enjoy chatting,' and with those final words she put down the receiver. This conversation could have clearly waited until tomorrow.

Stephanie was more interested in what she was going to wear to dancing. Salsa was "the sexy dance", so she had been told. Reaching into her top drawer, she pulled out a black, lacy top. *Perfect,* she thought to herself. She slid the top over her bust and smoothed it over her body. To finish tonight's outfit – her favourite silky skirt. It floated around her legs as she moved. Now for hair and makeup.

Stephanie sat in front of her mirror and turned on the curling wand. Waiting for the wand to heat up, she picked up her bright red lipstick and applied it to her lips. She added black mascara onto her long eyelashes and placed a tiny black dot on her cheek as a beauty spot.

A red light appeared to signal that the curler was ready. She smiled as she gazed into the mirror. Andrew would want her to do this too. He had suggested that she get back into dancing. Dancing was her new focus. It was becoming an addiction. Stephanie examined a curl that dropped past her shoulder. It did not seem to match the one on the other side. She began to curl it again. The other girls in the dance class always had their hair styled. When she did ballet, all the students wore their hair in a bun. In jazz class, dancers would have their hair pulled off their faces and out of the way, but in Latin dancing, all the girls seemed to let their hair dangle all over the place.

She had counted to ten again and released the curl. It sat perfectly this time. She wondered if Anton would notice her and her curls. *Surely he will …* she thought.

Standing in front of the mirror she twirled around in her skirt as it gracefully lifted around her. Her black semi-see-through lacy top revealed her bra but not in an obvious way. Stephanie put her mobile phone and wallet into her bag and decided to leave a note for her mum and dad.

I've gone to the dance class. See you when I get back. Love you, Steph x

She put on her black leather jacket and left the house. Melbourne could be so cold and wintry at any time of year. The door slammed behind her as she made her way down the path and onto the street.

Stephanie approached the traffic lights at the intersection of the highway. The train station was across the road. Cars roared past as she stood and waited by the red light.

A guy in a black long sleeved top stood next to her. He had just come out of the hotel. She could smell alcohol on his breath. He started to give her the eye. She looked away.

'Oi gorgeous, you have any spare coins?'

'No, I don't,' Stephanie muttered as she put her head down.

Cars stopped and the lights changed to green. He began to stroll across the road. The smell of petrol, burgers and chips lingered in the air as she passed the service station and a fast food store.

The guy who had approached her at the traffic lights was only a few metres ahead. Stephanie hoped he was not going to catch the train too but unfortunately he turned into the entrance.

On the platform, Stephanie stood next to another lady wearing a long coat, scarf and gloves. She did not want to stand by herself.

The train arrived and Stephanie entered the same compartment as the lady. Across the aisle, a man sat reading the newspaper. Next to him, a man and lady held hands and whispered into each other's ears. Stephanie looked at the couple. She smiled. It made her think of dancing. The sexy Salsa was on her mind. She gently tapped her feet on the ground marking out the dance steps and trying to remember Anton's words.

'You got any spare coins?' The drunken man was at it again.

'No, leave me alone.'

A young girl got up from her seat and made her way to the other end of the carriage.

'You're so rude. Stupid girl.'

Stephanie bit her fingernail and stared out the window. A hand touched her shoulder and she could smell alcohol again.

'You got any spare coins?'

Stephanie turned to see the red-eyed man standing in front of her.

'Sorry, you asked me before and I said I didn't.'

'Oh yeeee, that's right,' he slurred. Removing his shaky hand from her shoulder he made his way to the door.

Stephanie began to tremble in her seat and grind her teeth. She had noticed his blood shot eyes and smelt his terrible breath.

Looking around, she hoped no one was paying attention. She took a deep breath and tried to control the tremble in her hand.

'Finally, we're here,' the lady muttered to her friend.

Stephanie gazed out the window she could see the skyscrapers in the distance. Making her way out the door, she was glad to be getting off the train. The tremor in her hands had stopped as she walked along the tunnel to the exit barriers. The glowing lights of the city were visible. Stephanie sighed as she headed in the other direction towards the dance school.

Chapter Eleven

The train crossed the railway bridge as Stephanie headed towards the underpass. Colourful graffiti covered the walls. Stephanie gasped, noticing the man who approached her on the train was in front of her. Stephanie stopped for a minute wondering if she should continue walking. Her mouth became dry.

Watching from a distance, she noticed another man approaching him. Stephanie began to take small steps, keeping her distance. She could see the man reaching out his hand. Something had been exchanged between the two men and a few words spoken, nothing more. The men continued on their own way. The approaching man glared at Stephanie as he walked past, as if to say 'mind your own business'.

Looking away, Stephanie continued to walk on. She wondered if they had been involved in a drug deal. A long time ago she had seen a movie where a similar scene had occurred and the drug deal had happened so fast. On the news recently there had been a story about a huge drug bust in a suburb close to Richmond. Stephanie shivered but redirected her thoughts.

The large building on the corner had a queue of patrons waiting at the entrance. A bulky man with a black jacket controlled the queue. As she walked past, Stephanie heard loud music and smelt cigarette smoke and alcohol. Pulling her collar over the side of her face she hurried past the line. She did not have far to go.

Reaching the intersection of Swan and Church Street, Stephanie could see the yellow sign. She breathed a sigh of relief knowing she would see Anton soon.

'Back again, you must have enjoyed it.'

Stephanie handed her the money to the girl at the desk but did not reply. She was trying to spot Anton.

She took a seat as her eyes scanned the room. There he was, talking to another lady who had a foreign accent. She was tall with long, dark brown hair and her face was heavily covered in makeup. Her large breasts were bursting out of her top as she tried to wrap her arm around Anton. Stephanie looked at the floor.

A girl came and sat next to her. She had long auburn hair down to her shoulders. Her black-rimmed glasses rested on her nose.

'Hey! I'm Eve. Some people call me evil – just joking! What's your name?' she said with a wicked giggle and a twinkle in her eye.

Stephanie laughed awkwardly. 'Hey … I'm Stephanie.'

'You're new here, right? I think I saw you last night?'

'Yeah, last night was my first class.'

Eve leaned in closer, she did not want anyone to hear her.

'You must have enjoyed the class. I've only been coming for a few weeks. I'm in love with Anton. He's so sexy. Hey, don't tell anyone this but … ' Eve looked around making sure that people were not listening, 'I don't think he has a girlfriend.'

'Why do you think that?'

'I've been asking the other dancers questions, in a subtle way, of course. Anyway, if I do find out he has a girlfriend, I'll kill her ... '

Stephanie pulled away from Eve.

'You seem cool, Steph. I think you and I may have a lot in common.' Eve smiled widely.

Stephanie fidgeted in her chair. Eve glared at her.

'How did you find out about Anton's dance school?' Stephanie asked.

'I've a friend who comes now and then – Louise – I'll introduce you sometime. She works with my dad, that's how I met her.' Eve took a deep breath. 'I live with my dad. My mum left us after I was born. Dad's been through so many girlfriends since. Some have been on drugs ... one even bashed him.'

Stephanie gasped.

'Look at this!' Eve scrolled through her mobile phone for a moment before handing it over to Stephanie. She looked at it closely. Displayed on the screen was a photo of a man with brown hair and a black eye.

'This is what dad's ex did to him on Christmas Day last year. I was going to call the police but she ran out of the house.' Eve took a quick glance around the room. 'The current girl seems okay, I guess. He never has much time for me.'

'So, are you at school?' Stephanie wanted to change the conversation.

Eve pulled an unpleasant face. 'School! I go to school when I feel like it. I hardly ever show up. Dad and the teachers don't care if I'm there. There are at least 100 students in my year level. Shhhhh! Stop talking, here comes – '

'You're back ... ' Anton interrupted their conversation and was looking down onto the two girls.

Stephanie stood up trying to catch his eye.

'Yeah … I wanted to give it another go. I really love dancing.'

'Good for you.' Giving her a wink, Anton turned around and made his way to the back room.

'Not fair! He never speaks to me.'

Stephanie could hear the frustration in Eve's voice.

'I can't believe he noticed you!' she snapped. 'It took me over an hour to get ready. Damn!' She folded her arms in disgust. 'Maybe I should wear red lipstick. Damn, I'll get him to notice me somehow. It's just a matter of time. I hate the fact that dad sent me to an all-girls school. Anyway, I like older men.'

The music started playing, Eve grabbed Stephanie's arm and dragged her onto the dance floor. All the ladies tried to make their way to the front near the mirrors. Tam stood right behind Anton.

'What a show off, she's standing in my way,' Eve whispered into Stephanie's ear.

She moved to the side so she could have a clear view of Anton. The older lady who had been chatting to Anton before the class was in the front row with a huge grin on her face.

Anton looked into the mirror and stared right at Stephanie.

'Tonight we'll be going over the steps for the Salsa. Watch me first and then follow along.' With his hands he smoothed his hair behind his ears and observed himself in the mirror. Swaying his hips to the beat, he captivated his class. 'You try it now.'

Everyone in the room began to move to the beat. Stephanie continued to stare at Anton. Her mother had told her it was rude to stare but she had an excuse, she was learning to dance.

'That's enough,' Anton said.

Stephanie felt she had just been awakened from a dream.

'Girls on one side of the floor, boys on the other. Tam, come here, we'll demonstrate,' Anton commanded.

Eve positioned herself near Anton.

'Sorry, I was standing here first,' a girl told her.

'I'll just move across,' Eve replied.

Stephanie focused on Anton's toned, muscular body. She brushed her hair behind her ear and waited for the next song to start.

Anton stood proudly in the middle of the room holding hands with Tam. Counting to himself he then began to dance.

Watching them move, Stephanie wished she was dancing with him. She began to think about the last time she had danced with Anton, not wanting to let go of his hands. She had loved the way he had taken her by surprise when he twirled her to face the mirror.

Eve's eyes were glaring at Tam, watching every move she made. Tam was doing her best to stare into Anton's eyes.

'Now that everyone is watching, remember from last class I mentioned that the man always leads.'

Dancing around the room, Anton was the centre of attention, all eyes focused on him.

'Right, next we'll partner up, you know how it works.'

Stephanie's jaw dropped. She hoped he would choose her to dance with first.

Anton began to pair people up and position them around the room.

'I hope I get to dance with Anton first,' Eve whispered to Stephanie.

Stephanie nodded. 'Anton gets to decide.'

'You over there, Zara. Helena, you're with Con'.

He pointed in the direction they needed to go. Stephanie felt the dance studio was like a chessboard and Anton controlled where the pieces on the board were going to move. He had the power and control.

Many years ago, Stephanie's grandfather had taught her how to play chess. His wise words danced in her head.

'*Chess is a mind game where you need to outsmart your opponent. Stephanie, you don't want them to know what you're thinking. You need to be in control of the board and the pieces on it. Never let your guard down. Life can be a game of strategies too. Be careful about the moves you make and do not trust people easily.*'

'Eve, you're with Harvey,' Anton said.

An ageing, bald-headed man leered at Eve. Eve crossed her arms and wrinkled her nose but obeyed Anton. Harvey grabbed Eve's hand and pulled her closer to him.

Stephanie cringed as she watched Harvey with Eve. She waited for Anton to direct her to her dance partner. Looking around the room, she noticed that most of the men were at least 40 and above. Anton was definitely the youngest male.

'Stephanie, you're with Jacob,' Anton pointed at Jacob. Stephanie moved towards Jacob.

'How are you tonight?' he said as she stood in front of him.

'I'm well thanks, and you?'

'I think I'm starting to get the Salsa. I did learn it many, many years ago. Guess I'm showing my age.'

Anton made his way over to the CD player and started the music.

Stephanie shivered she hoped that she would be able to remember the steps. Jacob smiled and she returned his gesture.

'Remember, the man leads!' Anton called out as he returned to the dance floor.

The dance students mirrored Anton and Tam's moves.

Stephanie focused on her steps. Gliding along the dance floor, she tried to keep up. Jacob twirled her around and she found herself standing next to Eve and Harvey. Harvey was pulling Eve closer to his body.

'Everyone stop for a moment!' Anton commanded.

Stephanie was still looking at Eve and Harvey. Even though they had been told to stop, Harvey continued to move his hand up and down Eve's back. Again Stephanie cringed, something did not feel right. *Is Harvey taking advantage of Eve because she's a young girl?* Stephanie wondered.

'This is the way everyone should be doing this step. Watch as I twirl Tam around.' Anton and Tam moved closer to the mirror, making the step look so easy.

Stephanie watched them dance. Secretly she wanted to be the one dancing with Anton. Dancing with Jacob was not the same.

'The man must be so careful where he places his hand as this leads his partner and guides her into the next step. If my hand is above my head that shows my partner that I'm going to spin her under my arm.'

Tam ducked under Anton's arm and took two steps to the side.

'Very good, now change partners. Move to the next person in the circle.'

Stephanie squirmed she knew who was going to be her next partner. She swallowed at the thought of what may happen next. She had no control of the situation.

Anton pointed at Stephanie. 'Steph, you're now with Harvey. Eve, you're with me,' he said as his eyes scanned the room, making sure that everyone was where he had positioned them.

Stephanie tried to avoid eye contact with Harvey. She took a deep breath. Anton had made it clear that everyone had to dance with different people – there was no choice.

As she listened to the beat of the music, her feet began to move.

'Hello,' he muttered to her.

'Hi,' she replied.

'So … ' he continued.

'I can't hear you the music is too loud to talk.'

Stephanie's thoughts began to wander to a time when she had been a little girl playing in the backyard. The door to the house had blown shut in the wind and she had been locked out. Scared and upset, she did not know what to do. This is how she felt now.

'Stop!' Anton called out as he grabbed Stephanie's hand. 'Change partners.'

She breathed a sigh of relief finally she was getting to dance with him. This is what she had longed for the whole night, to have his skin touching hers. She tried to catch his eye but he did not look down. She could smell his musky aftershave as she swayed her hips.

'Stop!' Anton announced, still holding Stephanie's hand. 'Time to wrap it up.'

Stephanie sighed, that had been a short dance. Had she done something wrong and he no longer wanted to dance with her?

'Well, I hope you all enjoyed the Salsa. Make sure you practice at home. I'm going to put on some music for the people who want to stay back and practice,' he said as he looked deep into Stephanie's eyes. Her eyes met his and she slightly lost her balance.

'Be careful, Steph.' He gave her a wink and made his way off the dance floor.

Chapter Twelve

Standing in the middle of the dance floor, Stephanie sighed. Her body was hot and sweaty and her dark hair was now wet and had lost its curl.

'Didn't know how lost I felt till I found yooooou ... ' Zara was standing in front of the mirror swaying her body and singing. Her head kept turning in Anton's direction. The other girls had not left the dance floor either.

Stephanie huffed. She'd had enough and no longer wanted to be on the dance floor. She hurried to the bathroom.

She gazed at her reflection in the mirror - her now pink cheeks were a contrast to her previously pale complexion on arrival. Turning on the tap, Stephanie splashed the cool water over her hands and face. Shutting her eyes, she tried to relax. The sound of sobbing interrupted her. The noise was coming from behind the toilet door.

'Are you okay?'

The sobbing continued. Stephanie knocked on the door.

'Are you okay?' she repeated.

Stephanie stepped back from the door.

'It's Stephanie, can I help you?'

'Stephanie!' The door swung open and standing in front of her was Eve. Her face was flushed and covered in tears.

'I don't know what to do,' she sobbed. 'I need someone to talk to. Can we go for a coffee?'

The bathroom door flung open and an older woman walked in.

'Hey, you're new, right? I'm Helena.'

'Hi, yeah, I am. Nice to meet you. I'm Stephanie. Not sure if you know Eve – '

'We're not staying,' Eve butted in grabbing Stephanie's hand and pulling her through the doorway and across the dance floor. Many of the students were still standing around, their eyes focused on Anton.

'Bye girls!' Anton called as they walked passed him. Eve kept her eyes focused on the ground and did not look back. Her grip tightened on Stephanie's hand as she guided her down the stairs and into the street finally releasing her.

'Where should we go for coffee?'

'To be honest, I don't really know Richmond.'

Eve frowned. 'I'll find us somewhere to go. We must get away. The further away the better.'

Stephanie gulped she did not understand what Eve meant and she dared not ask.

The moon shone brightly in the dark sky as the two girls waited patiently for the tram.

'Here it comes.'

'About time!' Eve snapped. 'Hurry, let's go!'

Eve and Stephanie scanned their transport cards and found a seat.

As the tram screeched along, Stephanie glanced curiously out the window. She admired the historical buildings in Richmond.

It was an older suburb of Melbourne, close to the city. When her parents had spoken to her about Richmond they had mentioned it had large Greek and Vietnamese communities.

The Greek community ... Stephanie thought. Nicole quickly entered her mind. *I wonder if she's spoken to her dad about Jim?* Stephanie shook her head. *Nicole was so boy crazy!*

'Let's get off here,' Eve stood up. She grabbed Stephanie's hand and led her off the tram.

They had only past a few shops when Eve stopped again.

'This place will do,' Eve said as she pushed open the café door. 'Let's sit here. No one can see us at this table.'

Stephanie placed her bag on her lap. The wooden table had a small number 44 and a menu on it.

'I wonder if it's table service?' Eve had grabbed the menu. 'I'm going to get a hot chocolate. What about you?'

Stephanie's eyes scanned the café.

'Did you hear what I said?'

'Sorry,' she said, slightly taken back by the comment. 'I think I'll have a latte.'

Eve pushed out her chair. 'I'm going to wash my face Stephanie. Can you tell the waiter what I want?' With that, Eve left the table.

Stephanie touched her head, she was developing a thumping headache and the loud music was bothering her. She looked at her gold watch – *9.30 p.m.* It was getting late and she still had to catch the train home and go to work in the morning. A couple exited through the door and she wondered if she should join them. *Stop it, Steph,* she told herself. *How would you like to be treated like that? I can't ditch the girl.* Resting back into the chair, she called for the waiter and placed her and Eve's order.

'So, what do you think of Anton?'

'I'm not sure … Tonight was only my second class.'

'Why are you not sure? He's tall, muscular and has a sexy body. I just can't take my eyes off him.' Eve leaned in closer. 'You do like him I can tell … '

'He can dance well.' Stephanie bit her lip.

'Come on Steph. He's hot,' Eve snorted.

'Yeah, he's good looking – '

'I was upset that I only got to dance with him once tonight,' Eve interrupted. 'That's what I look forward to my whole week – dancing with him.' Her frown changed to a smile. 'If only he was my boyfriend.'

Stephanie bit her nail and looked at the floor. Anton was sexy, she had to agree with Eve, but would not dare to reveal this to anyone. This would have to be her secret.

'Every day I plan what I'll wear to dancing and how to style my hair. I find a space in my room and go over the dance steps. Do you do this too Steph?'

'Err … when I have time I try to work on the steps.'

'A hot chocolate and a latte,' the waiter said as he placed the drinks onto the table.

'Nice and hot like Anton,' Eve giggled.

Stephanie took a sip of her latte trying to relax. The warmth of the hot liquid slid down the inside of her throat. The jazz music playing in the background rang in her ears. She rubbed her eyes not really wanting to continue this conversation but she did not want to seem rude.

'So Eve, do you feel better now?'

'I felt angry when I saw Helena.'

Stephanie frowned.

'You know Helena! She came into the bathroom and introduced herself, everyone knows Helena,' Eve snapped. 'The

Spanish lady with the strong accent. She was trying to put her hands all over Anton before class. She's in *love* with him, it's so obvious!' Eve poked her finger into her mouth as if she was about to be sick. 'She's so much older. I've got more of a chance. Anyway, my plan is to kill her and Tam ...'

Stephanie sat back in her chair folding her arms.

'Tam is the Vietnamese girl who always demonstrates the dances. Are you listening?'

'I know who she is,' Stephanie replied.

'She pretends to be all pretty and sweet but I won't let her stand in my way.'

Stephanie glared at Eve. 'Uhh ... I'm not sure that's the best approach to take.'

Eve started to laugh. 'I'm only joking Stephanie, you didn't really believe me, did you?' Her brown eyes continued to stare into Stephanie's.

'Oh, of course not.' Stephanie reached for her coffee glass and took the last sip. 'Eve, I don't mean to be rude, but it's getting late ... ' Stephanie stood up from the table and placed her bag over her shoulder.

Eve frowned. 'That's okay. Let's swap mobile numbers before you leave so we can call each other?' Eve said as she handed over her mobile for Stephanie to enter her number.

Stephanie forced a smile and handed it back.

'Thanks for the chat, Stephanie. I'll give you a call soon. Oh, and don't forget to pay for your latte. I only have the right money to pay for my hot chocolate. I'm on a tight budget!'

Stephanie made her way to the counter, paid for her coffee and left. Taking a deep breath she was relieved to be walking out the door. She pulled her coat towards her chest and then looked at her watch – *10 p.m. already.*

The wild wind blew her hair as the street lights beamed over her casting a shadow. Deciding to walk, as there was no tram in sight, she hurried along the footpath as her shoes crunched on the fallen leaves.

The bright lights of a passing car shone into her eyes. *Why do people drive with their high beam on?* Stephanie thought. She was nearly at the dance school and noticed that the lights were still on in the studio. She wondered if Anton was having a private lesson.

Across the road, she could see a group of guys leaving the pub.

'Oh what a night, boys!' yelled one.

'Shame there were no hot birds though, ' slurred another.

'I know, right. Ugly bunch they all were, ha!'

The voices of the drunken men echoed in the night air. Holding her bag closer to her side, she did not look back. The voices started to fade as she continued along the street.

Stephanie could hear footsteps behind her, but kept walking. She picked up her pace as she passed the Mexican restaurant certain that someone, or something, was following her... Taking a deep breath, she quickly turned around.

Nothing. The vacant street stared back at her.

The wind blew a piece of rubbish at her feet. *I need to catch that train,* she thought. Reaching into her bag, she pulled out her mobile phone and continued to walk faster. Stephanie could hear footsteps again. Without thinking, she turned around. A tall, dark figure dashed into the side street. Someone had been following her.

The beam of a car's lights flicked across her body. It was a taxi. She waved her hand madly and the car stopped. She climbed in.

'10 Docker Street, Elwood, please.'

'Sure. How has your night been?' the young driver asked.

'Not too bad… Ready for bed now.'

'Friday night, no partying for you?'

'Not tonight, I was actually at a dance class. Then I went for coffee with a friend. I'm exhausted … Need to get home.'

'My last passengers were a group of girls I dropped them off at a bar. It's been pretty busy.'

'I'm glad to head home. I saw a group of drunken guys before.'

'I refuse to take drunk guys in my taxi – '

'Plus, I think someone was following me … I wouldn't usually walk the streets alone.' Stephanie interrupted.

'Richmond isn't a very safe area to walk around at night. It's close to the city and has lots of pubs. Anyway, the name's Lance.'

'I'm Stephanie. '

'Nice to meet ya, Stephanie. I'll give you my card, just in case you need a lift again, and you can call me direct. At least you know the driver then. I've a few clients I do this for. Mrs Lacy is one of my favourites, she's a sweet old lady in her eighties. Sometimes I take her to get her groceries.'

'Oh, thanks. That would be quite handy actually.'

'No worries. So … I assume you like dancing if that's where you were tonight … '

'I used to dance when I was younger, had a break and now trying Latin.'

'It's good to exercise. I go to the gym when I can. I've only been in Melbourne two years.'

'Where are you from?' Stephanie asked.

'Adelaide.'

'Why did you move?'

'I lived in Adelaide with my ex-girlfriend. It didn't work out so I thought I needed a change and moved here. Melbourne is a great place to live.'

'So did you drive a taxi in Adelaide?'

Lance started laughing. 'No, I use to work in sports management, mainly with athletes. Not sure if I'll drive taxis forever but it will do for now.'

The taxi stopped outside her place. Reading the meter, she paid the fare.

'Here's my card, Stephanie. If you need me to drive you somewhere.'

'Thanks. I think I may have to take you up on that offer.'

'No problem. Happy for you to,' he smiled. 'See you.'

Chapter Thirteen

Entering the house, Stephanie dropped her bag onto the table and placed the card from Lance next to it. There was a message on her phone.

Hi Stephanie, thanks for chatting to me. Can we meet tomorrow for a drink? I'll call you. Eve x.

Replying to that can wait, Stephanie thought.

'Mum? Dad? Are you home?'

Stephanie unbuckled her black shoes and placed them under the table. The pain in her legs became more intense as she wiggled her toes. Her black lacy top clung to her sweaty body. Staring at the kettle she was tempted to make a cup of tea but heating up some potato and leek soup seemed more appealing. She placed the bowl into the microwave and hit start. While she waited, she turned on her iPad to check her email.

One new email from Emma. The subject heading read, 'It's never too late'.

Hey Steph, hope the crystal ball session helped. Just wanted to remind you, it's never too late to find love. Try the dating app but if that doesn't

work, try something else. Life is to be enjoyed. See you soon xxxx

God, Emma can be so annoying sometimes … but I know she cares … and she's great for advice. Stephanie thought. She wondered if she should email her about the guy following her but decided it was easier to chat to her about it when she saw her next.

Stephanie closed her email, put her phone in her pocket and then carefully carried the soup bowl to the coffee table in the lounge room. Grabbing the television remote, she flicked through the channels. An English soccer game did not interest her neither did a cooking show. World news was not appealing. She just switched it off. Reaching for her mobile she remembered Emma chatting about the dating app. Stephanie typed Flirtnow in the search section of the App Store.

FLIRTNOW - DOWNLOAD IN SECONDS, EASY TO JOIN! FIND YOUR PERFECT MATCH WITH THE TOUCH OF A BUTTON.

Stephanie clicked on the green button and registered. Glancing at her watch she realised it was after midnight. *Time to get some sleep …*

Climbing into bed she switched off the bedside lamp. Aches and pains shot up her legs. She focused on the ceiling and then closed her eyes. Anton's voice started to play in her mind.

'*Salsa is the sexy dance …*'

She remembered standing on the dance floor and thinking it was like a chessboard. The words of her grandfather rang in her ears.

'*Be careful of the moves you make and don't trust people easily …*' *Never let your guard down … '*

Anton had controlled the floor telling his dance students where to move.

She could hear footsteps outside her door.

'Mum? Dad? Is that you?' Stephanie waited for a response. 'Mum, are you home?'

She could hear a dog barking in the street.

Throwing off the sheets, she walked out of the bedroom to the lounge area and into the kitchen. Had someone followed her?

She looked around the room. Coffee table, leather sofa, television – everything was still there. *Phew, no burglars,* she thought. Biting her lip, Stephanie drifted back into the hallway.

'Mum?'

'Stephanie?' Her mother appeared from the bedroom.

'You scared me!'

'Sorry darling, we just got home. Your father's gone straight to bed. He's so tired.'

'I wasn't sure if you were back. I actually thought someone may have broken in!'

'Everything's fine,' her mother reassured her. 'How was your night?'

'Yeah, okay. I got a taxi home, didn't want to be walking around the streets so late.'

'Sorry Dad couldn't pick you up from dancing. Getting the taxi was definitely a good idea. You don't want to be putting yourself in danger. Remember, you can always call Emma, she said that was fine.'

'Yeah, Mum. I know. I didn't think of Emma at the time. I don't mind catching a taxi if it's getting late. But I do want to keep going to dancing.'

'I think you should keep going too.'

Stephanie rubbed her eyes. 'I'm really tired. I'm going back to bed.'

'Here, give me a hug. Goodnight.'

'Goodnight, Mum.'

Stephanie climbed back into bed. She stared at the ceiling. Who had been following her in the street? And why …

She huffed. *Stephanie, you need to get some sleep.* Staying awake was not going to solve her problems.

Chapter Fourteen

'What are your plans for today?' Stephanie's mother asked from across the breakfast table.

'I'm not sure yet.'

'I'm planning on doing grocery shopping. Need anything?'

'Can't think of anything?'

'Just thought I'd ask. Might go soon.'

Stephanie nodded. 'That's okay, Mum. You don't have to worry about me. I might go out later and buy a new top for dancing.'

Stephanie took another sip of her coffee as her mother finished cleaning up the dishes on the bench.

'All done. Can you put your mug in the dishwasher when you've finished?'

'Sure.'

'See you later, love.'

Stephanie yawned, as she relaxed back into the chair. She could hear the sound of the tap dripping. All she could think about was dancing. What should she wear to the next class? Would she get to dance with Anton? Did he like her? It was hard to be sure. He had looked at her many times and even winked.

Stephanie huffed. *I need answers,* she thought. *Maybe I'll pay another visit to Madam Farrell …*

Her mobile began to ring. It was Eve. Stephanie bit her lip.

'Hello?'

'Hey, did you get my text?' Eve said.

'Yeah, I did. A few things happened and I forgot to reply, sorry.'

'Oh …' Eve did not seem convinced. 'Anyway, I was wondering if we could catch up today. I need someone to talk to.'

Stephanie took a deep breath. 'I would love to Eve but I have something already planned.'

'Really?' Eve said sarcastically.

'Well, I can chat to you now for a bit.'

'Mmmm … I guess that's better than nothing,' Eve breathed heavily into the phone. 'So … I want to become an actress. Last night I went online and searched for a talent agency. I found one but they have a joining fee.' She took a deep breath. 'This is where you come in, Stephanie … I can't tell my dad, let alone ask him for the money. I'm a bit short of cash. Can you lend me some?'

Stephanie raised her eyebrows. 'Uhh … Eve … I can't.'

'So you won't help me?'

'I don't have a lot of cash myself.'

'Can't you ask your parents? I'm going to start applying for after-school jobs. When I get one, I'll pay you back. I need to join this acting agency.'

'I don't ask my parents for money. I have a part-time job at the library – '

'Maybe you can just borrow some money and don't tell them?' Eve butted in. 'Then pay them back. Please, Steph, *pleeeeease* help me.'

'Eve, I can't do that. I think you should speak to your dad.'

'I can't!' Eve shouted down the phone. 'He … he hates me. He doesn't care about me. If I get into acting maybe Anton will notice me. Steph, when I met you, I knew you would be a good friend. Please help me. What should I do?' Eve started to sob into the phone.

'Don't cry, Eve. I think you need to rethink this. Maybe just concentrate on the dancing for a while and then get into acting? Maybe by then you'll have a job?'

'Why is life so hard, Stephanie? Why don't guys like me? I hate myself … '

'Don't feel like that, Eve.'

'I've got to go. I think Dad's just arrived home. I'll talk to you later. Bye.' Eve ended the call.

Stephanie gasped. *That was unexpected.* She grabbed her bag and left the house. Walking past her favourite coffee shop, she remembered the last time she had been there – it was with Andrew. *Life is not fair …*

The warbling sound of a black and white bird flying past caught Stephanie's attention. A bird was one of the images that Madam Farrell had seen in her crystal ball.

A bird, what could that mean? I have to see Madam Farrell, she thought. *It may help answer some questions.* Glancing at her watch she rushed to the station.

'The train from Elsternwick station will depart in five minutes,' a voice said over the loudspeaker.

Biting the top of her nails, Stephanie waited. The train came to a stop and she boarded.

A newspaper lay on the seat next to her. Resting her head

on the palm of her hand, she gently closed her eyes and remembered what Madam Farrell had said.

'Bird, cat and snake can be seen as symbols ...'

Symbolism and books, the lady who returned that book *The Undiscovered Worlds of Peru* mentioned that it was an interesting read.

The doors closed and Stephanie looked aimlessly out of the window, Ripponlea Station, Balaclava Station, Windsor Station, Prahran Station, South Yarra Station.

'The next stop is Richmond Station,' the recorded message announced.

The doors opened and Stephanie made her way along the platform and down the stairs.

Walking into Richmond through the underpass, she noticed the colorful graffiti on the walls and many poster advertisements for upcoming events. Cars raced by, honking their horns as they tried to speed past the tram. Loud voices could be heard from the corner pub as she strolled by. In the distance, Stephanie could hear the tinkling of chimes. She was nearly there.

Pushing aside the purple decorations that dangled in front of her face, she entered the crystal shop. The smell of lavender filled the room as she stood at the front desk. Burning candles lit the room.

'Stephanie, you're back.' A lady in a red robe stood in front of her.

'Madam Farrell, just who I wanted to see. Are you free now?'

'Yes, you're a lucky girl, it's been very quiet. I'm not sure if it's the weather that has been keeping people away or maybe that full moon last night.'

Stephanie gasped. 'Did you say there was a full moon last night?'

'Yes, there was. Are you okay, dear?'

'Yeah … I just wanted to come and see you.'

'Come, let's go to my room and we can look into the crystal ball.'

Meowwww …

'There you are, Midnight! He's been acting strangely since the full moon. It's like something is worrying him. Dear me, what's all this meowing about? Do you want Stephanie to give you a pat? He loves attention and people patting him. There was only one time when he didn't really like a fellow. He came into the crystal shop. I remember he had an accent and was quite abrupt. That night when Midnight lay on my bed, I had a strange dream about snakes. They were trying to attack Midnight. Midnight acted strangely for about a week after that. Funnily enough, it was around the full moon as well. Watch your step, this staircase is steep.'

The wooden door creaked as Madam Farrell leaned against it.

'Here, Midnight, sit on this cushion. Stephanie and I need to consult the crystal ball. Please take a seat, Stephanie.'

Stephanie's eyes were drawn to the crystal ball.

'I'm receiving a message, we need to play Latino music in this session and I'll burn some incense too.'

A tiny flame flickered in front of Stephanie.

'Right, I think we're ready.' Covering her hair with the red hood, her green eyes looked at Stephanie. 'Now shut your eyes and relax, sit up straight and take deep breaths in and out. I know why you're here. You want answers. I can see an image. Please don't speak.'

Stephanie waited patiently.

'A bird, a tall dark figure and a full moon. Now a cat and a snake have appeared. The bird is now flying right above the cat. Wait a minute the image is fading. You can speak now. How do you feel, Stephanie?'

'I'm so confused. Nothing makes sense. I saw a magpie on the way here maybe that's a sign. The cat and snake I cannot explain.'

'Try and relax, Stephanie. Take a deep breath.'

'What can you see, Madam Farrell?'

'I see a word. It says "sacrifice". To what this refers or means, I'm not sure. All I know is that the crystal ball can show current situations and future happenings. Stephanie, no more for today…You must go home. How did you get here?'

'By train.'

'You can't catch the train home. I'm feeling that's not safe.'

'I don't know if I should tell you this,' Stephanie said. 'But I think someone was following me yesterday. What do you think, Madam Farrell?'

'I'm not sure. The crystal ball does not let me know these things but I just have a feeling you shouldn't catch the train home.' Madam Farrell said as she removed her hood. 'Open your eyes when you're ready.'

'I'll call a taxi,' Stephanie rested her elbows on the table.

'Midnight!'

The black cat jumped onto Stephanie's lap. He felt warm as he brushed against her arm. Nuzzling into Stephanie's body, the cat began to purr.

'This is a sign, Stephanie. You were the cat in the crystal ball. The animals represent people.' Her eyes widened as she spoke. 'I'm unsure who the bird and snake are at this stage. It will take time for us to find this out. Go home, you must go home, before it gets dark.'

Stephanie placed the bundle of fur onto the floor. 'How much do I owe you?'

'This was a short session, just make it $40, thank you. And Stephanie, remember to trust your gut.'

Placing the notes into Madam Farrell's right hand, she smiled and made her way down the stairs.

Chapter Fifteen

Stephanie scrambled around in her bag looking for Lance's card. *Damn, where is it …* she thought.

Looking down the street, she spotted a taxi that was dropping off a passenger. She waved at the car.

'Hello. To Elwood, please.'

'Sure,' the taxi driver replied.

'I'm so glad I saw your taxi and didn't have to call one.'

The interior of the taxi smelt like stale cigarettes. She wound down her window and took a gulp of fresh air.

'Where in Elwood are you going?'

'Can you drop me off in the shopping strip.'

'No worries.'

Stephanie stared out the window she did not wish to continue the conversation.

Twenty minutes later, they arrived at the shopping strip. Stephanie handed over the money.

'Thanks, gorgeous. So … what are you up to now?'

'Meeting a friend.' She could see the driver glancing in his mirror, it really was none of his business.

'I see … well, enjoy your night.'

Stephanie shook as she left the car. She hoped the driver

would not follow her. Peering over her shoulder she noticed he had not driven away. She hurried along the shops as the wind whipped against her body, turning the corner she dug deep into her bag finding her house keys, opened the door and went inside.

Symbols, people, Latin music, dancing, these were all thoughts drifting in her mind after her meeting with Madam Farrell.

Walking into the lounge area, she noticed the book on the floor. Stephanie stared at the gold letters – *The Undiscovered Worlds of Peru*. She picked it up and began to read. Her eyes skimmed the index page stopping at the word 'sacrifice', 'humans', 'gods' and 'animals'. She continued reading.

The sun and moon are highly regarded by the Incas. Gold is linked to the sun and represents males whereas silver is linked to the moon and represents females. Both the sun and moon control the sky in turn from day to night.

Stephanie turned the page, a heading read 'Gods'.

The Incas believed strongly in humans giving back to the gods, sacrifices were common in their world.

Stephanie held the book tightly as she read over the last six words, sacrifices were common in their world. She swiftly turned the page.

It was believed that three worlds constantly interacted. A bird represented the world of the gods, a cat represented the living world and a snake represented the world of the dead and the ancestors below.

Had she just read about birds, cats and snakes? Stephanie gasped and quickly shut the book.

Her mobile screen lit up. One message received from Eve.

Hi Steph, what's going on?

Stephanie messaged back.

Not much. I feel a bit sick, just resting.

Eve replied within seconds.

Take some drugs to help. That helps me feel better. Can I call now?

Stephanie typed back.

Yeah.

Within a minute of her replying, her phone began to ring.

'Hello?'

'Hey, my dad's gone to get some petrol so I can talk to you for a bit.'

'How are you feeling?' Stephanie asked.

'I've been thinking. I know what to do now. I'm going to focus on dancing for awhile then get into the acting. I have to get serious about job hunting,' Eve whispered. 'What do you think?'

'I think that sounds like a good idea.'

'Stephanie, I'm so glad I've met someone like you. I've only really ever had one friend, Annie. When Annie had to move to

Geelong with her mum I was devastated. I cried for weeks and weeks.'

'Why did she move to Geelong?'

'Her parents got divorced. Her dad was an alcoholic. I remember going over to her house and her dad would be screaming at her mum.' Eve took a deep breath. 'Her dad seemed okay. Our dads used to have a couple of beers together when she was over at my place. I miss her so much.' Eve went silent.

'Eve, at dancing you can meet new people and make friends.'

'Yeah, I met you. And the man I want to marry, Anton. But I have to work on my new look so Anton will notice me,' Eve groaned.

'New look? What do you mean …'

'Talk to you about it later. I gotta go. Sorry, bye!' Eve ended the call.

'Stephanie, you're home,' her mother said cheerfully as she entered the room.

'I've been here a while.'

'Ah, didn't hear you. Would you like something to eat?'

Stephanie yawned, quickly covering her mouth. 'I'm not feeling the best again.'

'Oh darling, can I do anything to help?'

'I'm just going to take a Panadol and have a rest.'

'Sure, sweetheart.'

Stephanie headed for the bathroom. Her pale face was reflected in the mirror. She opened the cupboard and found the painkiller. Placing the white tablet on her tongue, she swallowed. Stephanie collapsed onto the bed.

The sound of her bedside alarm frightened her.

There was no way Stephanie could go to work feeling like this. She would have to call the library.

'Hampton library, Alison speaking, how may I help you?'

'Hi Ally, it's Stephanie. Just ringing to let you know I'm not feeling too well ... don't think I'll make it in today.'

'Oh, poor thing, that's no good. No stress, take the day off and we'll see you Monday.'

Stephanie breathed a sigh of relief.

'Thanks so much, Ally.'

'No worries, Stephanie. Take it easy, get some rest and go and visit the doctor.'

Stephanie got herself a glass of water and rested on the couch. She hoped Eve would not call today. Picking up the remote control, she flicked through the channels. There was nothing on as usual. So she reached for her mobile instead.

The screen lit up as she touched the dating app. She entered her email address.

Stephanie's eyes were drawn to the 'Hot or Not' button. Curious as to what it was all about, she clicked the button. Within seconds, hundreds of pictures of smiling males, all around her age, flooded her mobile screen. As she scrolled through the handsome – and not so handsome – faces, she noticed the swipe tool that sat below each photograph. Swipe left for 'No, I'm not interested' or swipe right for 'Yes, I'm interested.'

Wow, thought Stephanie. *That's easy.*

The first guy that caught Stephanie's eye had black hair, olive skin and dreamy eyes - Adam. He looked similar to Andrew and Anton. The only difference was he had straight hair, not curls.

I'll give him a go, Stephanie thought as she swiped right.

A ginger-haired guy with a cheery smile captured her interest - Brad. He looked friendly so Stephanie swiped right again. *Just one more for now ...*

A blonde-haired, blue-eyed male was next. He looked a little shy - his gaze was not directed at the camera.

Hmmm ... Daniel. Right swipe for you. Stephanie stared at the screen. *What am I doing? I've not dated for so long,* she thought. *Am I ready for this?*

She put down her phone and leaned back into the chair.

The room was silent, apart from the clock ticking on the kitchen wall and the buzz of her laptop being charged. She started to tremble. Why was she feeling like this? Suddenly single, she didn't know how to replace the hole in her heart. The silver bracelet, Andrew's birthday gift, had not left her wrist. She wished she could have said goodbye. Stephanie missed the way he held her in his arms and his gentle kiss on her lips.

Her mobile phone began to ring - blocked number.

'Hello, Stephanie speaking?'

'It's Eve, Stephanie. I need to talk to you. Can we meet now?'

'Hey, is everything okay? I'm meant to be at work but I wasn't feeling the best so I didn't go'.

Eve took deep breaths down the other end of the phone.

'Are you okay, Eve?'

'No, I'm not,' she snapped back and hung up.

Stephanie's hand began to tremble. Before she knew it, she was calling Eve's mobile. The phone rang and rang. Finally, Eve picked up.

'Hello?'

'Eve, I'm worried about you... Let's meet up for a chat, near the dance school?'

'Yeah, okay. I'll meet you soon.'

The feel of her soft velvet robe was comforting and the last thing she wanted to do was leave the house. Yet, she had made a promise to Eve and promises had to be kept.

Stephanie quickly brushed her hair and in less than ten minutes she was ready to leave the house. Wearing her favourite blue jumper and jeans she picked up her bag. As she did this, she noticed Lance's card on the table. *That's where that went!* she thought as she picked up the card and put it in her wallet.

Chapter Sixteen

'Where are you?'

'Just at Richmond Station, Eve. I'll be there soon.'

'I'm waiting for you. I don't like standing here by myself Hurry up.'

Stephanie rushed down the stairs onto the street. As she walked she glanced at her watch. In the distance she could see Eve standing outside the Mexican restaurant.

'I didn't want to wait at the dance school just in case I saw Anton … '

Eve looked down at the pavement, her glasses nearly slipping off her nose. 'Stupid glasses! They make me look ugly … '

'I think they make you look smart.'

'Smart?' Eve snapped. 'I don't want to look smart.'

'What's wrong with being smart?'

'Look at you, dark hair and all … I have to work hard on my looks.'

'Eve, it's what's inside that counts.'

'Stephanie … I'm so in love with Anton and I'll do anything to have him.' She opened her wallet. 'Take a look at this.'

Stephanie's eyes focused on a picture of a man with dark hair, sparkling eyes and a huge grin. It was Anton.

'I carry Anton's picture with me everywhere.'

Stephanie handed the wallet back to Eve.

'Let's go to a coffee shop,' Eve suggested. 'I saw one on my way here.'

Stephanie nodded as they continued to walk.

Eve headed for a table at the back of the café. Stephanie followed behind.

'I don't want anyone to see us,' Eve said.

Stephanie pulled out her chair, something did not feel right. Again, Madam Farrell's words replayed in her head.

'Trust your gut … '

'We need to discuss the dance school. I should have mentioned this to you the last time we had drinks,' Eve said before leaning in closer. 'Harvey is a strange man.'

Stephanie nodded. 'I've noticed.'

'When I was dancing with him, he was trying to feel me, reaching his hand around my body and rubbing it up and down me.'

'How awful!' Stephanie gasped.

Eve closed her eyes. 'He was taking advantage of me but there was nothing I could do.'

Stephanie touched the lump that was starting to form in her throat. 'Eve, that's really bad. You have to tell Anton.'

'No!' Eve smashed her fist down on the table. 'Anton can't know about this.'

'Why?'

'My chances will be wrecked with him if I tell. You can't tell anyone about this,' Eve said sternly as she stared into Stephanie's eyes.

Stephanie shivered. *Is she threatening me?*

'It's our secret. Got it?'

Stephanie nodded.

Eve sat back in her chair. 'Now to the next issue ... I need to get rid of my competition.'

'What do you mean, Eve?'

'I mean the other ladies who like Anton. Some of the girls are like leeches.'

'In what way?'

'They hang around after class just hoping to spend more time with him. That's one thing I've noticed.'

'I've seen them do that.'

Eve groaned. 'There's so much competition. It's quite bitchy. Everyone wants to outdo each other.'

Stephanie sighed. 'I want to dance.'

Eve started to giggle. 'We all want to do that too. Anyway, I was thinking of ways to get rid of them.'

Stephanie cringed, thinking she needed to leave.

Eve started laughing. 'I'm not serious, my dad calls me evil Eve but I would never do that. I just mean how should I get Anton to notice me?'

'Sorry Eve, I don't think I'm really the person you should ask. I'm not an expert on dating.'

Eve ignored her comment. 'I need to get some new tops to show a bit of bust.' She pulled at her top a little.

'The problem is, Dad and I have no cash ... we can barely pay our rent.' Eve moaned. 'I might have to try the opportunity shop. Stuff this,' she threw her serviette on the table. 'Dad is so focused on his girlfriends. Big bunch of druggies they are. I'll show them all someday.'

She rested her chin on her hand as she glanced around the room.

Stephanie bit her lip.

'I know what to do,' Eve muttered.

'That's good,' Stephanie tried to avoid eye contact.

'Anyway, back to my competition ... You know that older Spanish lady who always has her bust showing?'

'Yeah.'

Eve pulled at her top again. 'Maybe I should show mine off too and then there's Tam, the Vietnamese girl, she's also a worry. She's always trying to stare into Anton's eyes.'

Stephanie politely nodded and pretended to be interested.

'I nearly forgot.'

'Forgot what?' Stephanie raised her eyebrows.

'My biggest competition ... you!'

Stephanie gasped. 'Eve!'

'Come on, Stephanie! I've seen the way you look at Anton.'

'I don't know what you are talking about.'

'Just kidding. I wanted to see how you would react. Zara is the one I'm most worried about. She's tall, skinny and looks like she has just stepped out of a Hollywood movie,' Eve muttered. 'Zara is definitely the one to watch. There's something about her.'

Stephanie squirmed in her seat.

'Maybe I should befriend Zara. That may work, Stephanie. I need time to think about it.' Eve looked at her mobile phone. 'Far out, is it 2 o'clock already? I have to leave, Dad will be angry with me. Thanks for the chat.'

She grabbed her bag and raced to the door.

Gee, thought Stephanie. *Not even a goodbye.*

'Excuse me, could I please order a coffee?' Someone new had arrived at the café.

'Sure. Is that take away?'

'Yes.'

Stephanie had heard that voice before. A hand touched her shoulder.

'Steph, what are you doing here?' Anton's brown sparkling eyes gazed into hers as he grinned with his pearly white teeth.

'I met a friend here.'

'Friend, meaning male friend?' his eyes widened as he spoke.

'No, just one of my girlfriends … Eve, actually.'

'Eve … '

'Yes, Eve,' Stephanie said with a smile. 'Would you like to join me for a coffee?'

Anton avoided eye contact. 'Got to go now, Steph. I'm organising a social night for the dance school on Saturday.' He smiled widely. 'I know it's late notice. I'll get Becky to call you. Actually, do we have your number?'

'I don't think so,' Stephanie bit her nail.

Anton reached into his pocket and pulled out his phone. 'Here, save your number.'

Stephanie took a deep breath. Her hand was shaking as she typed in the digits. Handing the phone back to him, she smiled shyly.

'Thanks Steph,' he said with a wink.

Stephanie played with her curl.

'I'm off. See you around.'

'Bye … '

She watched him grab his coffee and leave.

A hand moved in front of Stephanie's face as the waiter returned to the table.

'Another coffee?'

'No thanks.'

'No worries, Miss. Oh, and Miss, just watch out for that guy.'

Smiling at her, the waiter left the table.

Stephanie huffed. *What does that mean?* she wondered. Grabbing her bag, she charged over to the counter.

'Were you sitting over there?' the lady at the counter asked Stephanie.

'Just at that table at the back, thanks,' Stephanie said as she handed over the money. She looked around the coffee shop. 'Oh, one question … where's the waiter that served me? I need to ask him something.'

'Oh, Peter? He just left, done for the day. Anything I can help with?'

'Never mind, thanks anyway.'

As Stephanie walked to the door, she thought about Harvey and whether she should tell Anton about his behaviour. He made her feel uncomfortable too. Her father had always encouraged her to stand up for herself.

'Don't change the person you are just to fit in, Steph. In the long run, people will respect you for being you. Believe in yourself …'

Her father's words echoed in her mind as she walked towards Dance Discovery.

Stephanie peered into the distance. She could see a skinny girl with long hair standing out the front of the dance studio. The girl had her arm around a guy's shoulder. As Stephanie got closer she realised it was Zara and Anton. She watched as the two of them went inside. She knew in her heart that it was none of her business but she had to go inside, she needed to talk to Anton.

The large studio was empty and in darkness. Standing at the front desk, she wondered what she should do.

'Take this, I hope that will give you a lift.'

A loud voice was coming from the back room. Anton appeared with Zara. His arm was around her shoulder and she was gazing into his eyes. The two of them began to walk across the dance floor. Zara swayed her hips and flicked her hair.

'Stephanie, what are you doing here?'

'I just wanted to talk to you about something.'

Anton switched on the lamp at the front desk and turned to Zara.

'Let me know how it goes.'

She started to giggle. Anton played along.

'Miss Hollywood, ha ha! You better leave now.'

Gazing into his eyes, she smirked. 'I've got a comfy couch at home. I'll let you know how this goes, Anton.'

Zara twirled her hair around her finger as she left leaving a trail of perfume behind her.

Anton turned to Stephanie his eyes looked her up and down. 'I like what you're wearing. Blue is my favourite colour.' He held her hand and led her to the centre of the dance floor. 'I notice you had a little bit of trouble with one of the steps the other night. Put your hand on my shoulder. Relax your shoulders.'

Gently placing her left hand on his right shoulder, Stephanie tried to relax.

'Steph, keep your head up. You're getting spaghetti arms. You need to watch your frame. Just wait there a minute.'

Anton left her standing under a light beam. She stared into the mirror.

A sweet melody began to play. The gentle beat echoed in her ears. A blue light caught her face as Anton made his way back to join her on the dance floor. She took a deep breath. Placing her hand back onto his shoulder, she gazed into his eyes. Anton began to sway his body from side to side. His brown eyes sparkled as a smile appeared on his face. Stephanie allowed her body to move with his. She smiled sweetly in response. And in that moment, Anton began to sing.

'Never, ever, ever, felt as I do tonight. Look at my eyes they're shining bright. Oh yeah! I have been waiting for this moment to ask you to dance. I'm looking for a little romance. You take my breath away.

Never seen you wearing the colour, blue. It matches your eyes too and makes me mesmerised.

Lady in blue … my heart beats for you. Do you feel it too? There's nobody here. There's nothing to fear … when I am near.

Dancing with you, this is what I want to do. I don't want to let go of you tonight.

Never, ever, ever felt as I do tonight. Look at my eyes they're shining bright. Oh yeah! I have been waiting for this moment to ask you to dance. I'm looking for a little romance. You take my breath away.

Lady in blue … my heart beats for you. Do you feel it too? There's nobody here. There's nothing to fear … when I am near. Dancing with you, this is what I want to do.

I don't want to let go of this lady I'm with tonight. I'll never forget the way you made me feel tonight.

Lady in blue, lady in blue, lady in blue. I'm meant for you. Never, ever, ever, felt like this but I do tonight.'

The music came to an end and Anton stopped dancing.

'You've got a beautiful smile, Stephanie,' Anton cooed. His eyes were sparkling.

Chapter Seventeen

'Anton, I need to tell you something … '

His brown eyes stared into hers as he leaned in closer.

Biting her lip, she stared back at him.

'What is it?' Anton grabbed her right hand.

'There's a guy in the dance school who is behaving in a sleazy way.'

'Who?' Anton let go of her hand.

'It's Harvey.' Stephanie looked away.

'What's he doing?'

'I was talking to Eve. She's really uncomfortable with the way Harvey's been behaving.'

Anton smoothed his hair. 'Tell me more … '

'He's been holding her and … rubbing his hand up and down her back.'

Anton frowned. 'It happens a lot in the dance world. Just tell him you don't like it when he does it. Think about it, if you have a friend who's doing something you don't like, don't you just tell them?'

Stephanie sighed. 'Mmm, don't know really.'

'Just remember what I said, Steph,' cautioned Anton. 'And tell Eve the same thing. She's very young. It doesn't surprise me that she doesn't know how to handle these situations.' Slightly rolling his eyes, he turned his back and walked away.

Stephanie stood alone on the dance floor.

A man carrying a black bag appeared at the top of the stairs.

'What do you want?' he said in a foreign accent. He placed the bag on top of the front desk.

'I was just talking to Anton. I'm leaving now.' Stephanie headed for the stairs.

'You mean, Antonio,' he said sharply.

'I thought his name was Anton?'

'I call him Antonio. That was his name in South America. I'm his older brother Bruno.'

Bruno held out his hand. Stephanie reached forward to shake it but instead he quickly twisted her wrist and kissed the back of her hand.

'Pleased to meet you,' he said.

Her eyes were drawn to his left arm. She could see a large tattoo through his thin shirt.

'We're supposed to be closed … that's why I asked if I could help you. Anton never tells me what's going on. Do you dance here?' He placed his hand on her shoulder.

'Yes, I've started doing the group classes.'

He began looking up and down her body.

'I'm a bit of a dancer myself,' he muttered.

'What's going on?' Anton said as he made his way back into the room.

'I'm just meeting one of your dance students, bro.'

'Steph, we're closing up now.'

'Sorry, I was just on my way out.' Stephanie turned her back and made her way down the stairs. Her eyes started to water.

'See you next class!' Anton shouted.

Heavy raindrops ran down Stephanie's cheeks and onto her jumper as she walked. She began to shiver and started coughing. A lady under a bright colourful umbrella walked past her. The tree branches swayed in the wind and the rain drizzled down onto the parked cars.

Anton's words kept ringing in her ears.

'Lady in blue, my heart beats for you, do you feel it too?'

She paused for a moment. Feeling short of breath, she leaned against a wall. Her hands began to tremble and she wanted to burst into tears. Stephanie took a deep breath as she saw a truck roaring down the street just as a car was making a U-turn. She could hear the sound of the truck's tyres sliding on the wet road.

A loud scream came from a lady across the road. The white car was tilted on its side and something lay next to it. It was a body. Thick blood trickled from the unconscious person's mouth. Stephanie gasped. She could see the truck driver's head lying on the dashboard. He was not moving. The truck's headlights shone brightly onto the road. A man ran out of the food store and another couple had run over to the accident. A siren could be heard in the distance. A white car with flashing red and blue lights appeared from around the corner and stopped next to the accident. Two men dressed in navy blue uniforms got out and made their way over to the accident. Stephanie could not watch this anymore. Turning her back, she continued walking towards the train station.

The wind blew her scarf as she rearranged it around her neck. The pain in her head was increasing. She wanted to throw up. I need to call Lance, she thought.

Stephanie looked into her bag pulled out her mobile and his card. Next she punched in the numbers. The dial tone rang in her ear as she held the phone.

'Yellow Transport Taxis, Lance speaking.'

'Hi Lance, it's Stephanie. You gave me your card the other day, I took a ride with you in Richmond?'

'Ah yes, I remember. How's it going, Stephanie?'

'I'm okay. I'm just in Richmond, around the same area I met you last time. Do you think you could drive me home?'

'Sure. I'll probably be about ten minutes, I'm near the Melbourne Cricket Ground. The traffic is moving slowly. I think it may have something to do with this weather. Tell you what, are you near the Mexican restaurant?

'Yeah, it's not far.'

'I'll pick you up from there. See you soon.'

'Cheers.'

Stephanie hurried to the front of the Mexican restaurant. Shivering, she stood in the entrance so that she was sheltered from the rain.

A car drove past and its tyres splashed water into the air. Luckily, Stephanie was not close enough to get sprayed. A yellow taxi pulled into the curb. It was Lance. *Thank goodness,* she thought.

Stephanie opened the back door and climbed into the taxi. The warm air was comforting as she put on her seat belt.

'So, to Elwood?' Lance looked over his shoulder in Stephanie's direction.

'Yes please.'

'How have ya been?'

'Not the best … I just witnessed a car accident.' Stephanie stopped talking.

'Oh dear. I'm not surprised though. There are some crazy drivers out there. The roads are so slippery with all this rain. What happened?'

Stephanie adjusted her seat belt as Lance began to drive.

'A truck was driving along the main road and a car did a U-turn. The truck couldn't stop and crashed straight into it. Then the police arrived and other people rushed over to the scene ...' Stephanie paused to take a breath. 'I felt sick so I thought I'd call a taxi.'

'I don't blame you for not wanting to hang around the scene.'

'Someone I know got hit by a car ... ' Stephanie muttered.

'That's terrible. What happened?'

'He's ... I don't really want to talk about it.'

'Fair enough,' Lance said before quickly changing the subject. 'The weather is terrible. I wonder when this rain will ever stop. How is the Latin dancing going?'

'Yeah, I guess I'm enjoying it.'

'Guess?'

'Well, I like the dancing but my teacher, he's ...' Stephanie paused.

'What? Hasn't done anything bad to you, has he?'

'No, no. He's just so up and down. One day he's nice and the next he's not particularly friendly, actually quite rude. All the girls are in love with him...'

Lance stared into the mirror. 'Ha, ha, maybe I should come along sometime and see what this guy is like?'

'Well, he's having a social night soon. I don't know all the details yet.'

'I don't know any male dancers. I've never danced. Do many guys go to the class?'

'Mainly girls.'

'Single girls?' Lance asked with a chuckle.

'Not sure really... think most are...'

'Do you have a boyfriend?'

'I did … but not anymore.' Stephanie looked away.

'Yeah, don't miss my ex in the slightest … but a friend said I should try dating again. Apparently there's this new dating app … "Love Now" or something … can't remember –'

'Flirtnow?' Stephanie interrupted.

'Yeah, that's the one! Don't know how I feel about the whole "online" thing though. I met my ex at the gym.'

Stephanie bit her nail. 'Yeah, I met my ex at school.'

'Fair enough. Well, here we are.'

Stephanie checked the meter and paid the fare.

'Thanks heaps.'

'No worries, anytime,' Lance replied, flashing a wicked, white smile.

Stephanie couldn't help but find Lance a little attractive. She wondered how old he was. *Hmm, mid twenties perhaps.* Her thoughts instantly turned back to Anton. She sighed.

Chapter Eighteen

Splashing in the puddles, Stephanie reached the front door. She took off her damp jumper and sat on the couch.

'Steph, you're home. How was your day, love?'

'Yeah, not bad. Popped into Dance Discovery for a bit.'

'Oh, wonderful. How's it all going?'

'Really good. Latin American dancing is so different to what I'm used to though.'

Stephanie's mother sat next to her. 'I love the *Strictly Ballroom* movie. I could watch it over and over again,' her mother said. 'Does your dance teacher look like Scott by any chance?'

'He's tall and has dark hair.'

'That's a good start.'

Stephanie rubbed her eyes. 'He doesn't remind me of Scott but I actually feel a bit like Fran sometimes, a real beginner dancer.'

'Don't be so hard on yourself, Stephanie. This is something new and exciting. Like Fran, you'll learn quickly. You know how to dance.' Her mother's words were encouraging.

'The movements are all in the hips for the Salsa. It's so different.'

'You'll just have to practice them.' A smile appeared on her mother's face. 'What do they say in *Strictly Ballroom*? "Feel the rhythm"?'

'Mum ... ' Stephanie laughed.

'Maybe we should watch the movie again sometime. I think we have it on DVD. I want to watch Scott dance again. So what's your dance teacher's name?'

'Anton,' Stephanie said awkwardly, not knowing where to look.

'That's not a common name. Maybe we can nickname him Scott?'

'Mum!'

'Oh I'm joking, Stephanie. Anyway, the main thing is you're getting back into dance and I think that's great. In a few weeks you'll have to show me some steps.'

Stephanie nodded. 'Yeah, it will be a few weeks.'

'I can wait. Better get the dinner ready.'

'Mum, do you mind if I ask Emma over tonight?'

'Of course not, love. Go ahead.'

'Thanks.'

Stephanie could hear the wild wind outside and the rain hitting the window. Glancing at her mobile, she wondered if she had any matches on Flirtnow. *Hmm, should really text Emma first,* she thought.

Em, if you are free, drop by my place? x

Stephanie opened the Flirtnow app. *Wow, a match! Buzzzzzzz!*

Her mobile vibrated frantically. *Emma already?*

I've worked out my plan to get Anton to notice me. I'm sooooo happy. See you at dancing! Love your bestie, Eve xxx

Stephanie had to read the text over again. *What is she planning?* Not wanting to appear rude, Stephanie texted back.

Thanks for your text. I hope you're feeling a bit better now.

She returned to the Flirtnow app and read her notifications. The app had informed her of a new match. A blonde-haired, blue-eyed guy named Daniel had swiped 'yes' too.

HEY STEPHANIE, I'M GOING TO BE TOTALLY HONEST - WHEN I SAW YOUR PICTURE, I WAS INSTANTLY DRAWN TO YOU. I'M A LAWYER SO MY DAYS ARE OFTEN LONG AND IT'S A LITTLE DIFFICULT TO MEET PEOPLE. BUT I'D REALLY LIKE TO MEET YOU. PLEASE TELL ME MORE ABOUT YOURSELF. DANIEL X

Buzzzzzzz!
It was her phone again. Stephanie's eyes focused on the number. It was not Emma's.

Hey Steph, Anton here, details about Saturday night. Starts 8:30pm Rendezvous Restaurant 400 Church Street Richmond, tickets are $20. Hope to see you there.

She gasped and replied straight away.

Thanks so much, Anton. I'll be there :)

Her finger hit the send button. Seconds later, she received a reply.

Happy to hear that, see you soon :)

Buzzzzzzz!
Another message. *Anton again?*

Be there soon. E xx

Cool, see you soon.

'Mum, Emma will be here soon!' Stephanie called out.

She rested on the red silk cushions and shut her eyes. A vision of Anton appeared in her head …

Stephanie's arms wrapped around his body, all she wanted to do was kiss his lips. He grabbed her hand and led her through a doorway. Where was he taking her? She had Anton all to herself. They came to a stop and Anton reached his hand over to gently touch her face. His hand moved its way down her body and then he started to pull at her bra strap. One strap dropped off her shoulder, as he worked his way towards the other. Her skirt hit the floor and Anton's body leaned in closer towards her.

'Steph … '

Stephanie opened her eyes. Emma was standing at the end of the sofa.

'Hi Em.'

'Your mum let me in. You look tired?'

'I had a headache so I was just resting.' Stephanie sat up and made a space for Emma.

'Ah, that's no good.'

'It feels a bit better now though. So what have you been up to? Stephanie inquired.

'I've been on Flirtnow. Oh! Been meaning to ask, how's it going for you?'

'It's interesting.'

'Steph! What does that mean?'

'I got a match.'

'How exciting! Do tell.'

'His name's Daniel, he's a lawyer.'

'Oh! I like him already! Tell me more – '

'Dinner girls!' interrupted Stephanie's mother.

The two girls sat at the kitchen table. The steam rose as Jane placed the soup bowl in front of Emma.

'I'll leave you two alone.'

'Thanks so much, Jane.'

'You're welcome.'

'Okay so back to Flirtnow. I'm so glad you've joined. There are so many men to choose from, even if Daniel isn't the one. So how many guys did you swipe 'yes' to?'

'Three. And you?'

'Many.' A cheeky grin appeared on Emma's face. 'When I first joined, at least twenty.'

'Em … I could only handle three … so that's what I've started with … I don't want to take more than I can handle.'

'What about the other two?'

'Not sure yet, I've only seen the match from Daniel.'

'It's about putting yourself out there and taking risks, if you never try how will you ever know? Steph, you're a lovely girl who deserves the best. You just need to believe and trust in yourself.'

'I guess.' Stephanie nodded.

'Chatting to guys this way allows them only to see your profile picture. They can't judge your figure. I know I'm overweight and if I turned up at a bar I don't think I would get a look.'

'Don't say that.'

'I know I'm not the first girl the guys would look at.' Emma sighed.

'That's silly. Emma you're great. If they don't like you, they aren't worth it.'

'That's true. Oliver is so lovely.'

'Tell me about him!'

'He loves music, he's funny. Wait, Steph, I have an idea…'

'What's that?'

'We should do a double date! That would be fun!'

'I've just started chatting to Daniel … '

'Come on Steph, it's better to meet them and we can do this together.'

'Okay.'

'I'm excited! I'm going to send Oliver a message now.'

'Now?'

Emma tapped on her phone. 'Sent. Your turn.'

'What do I say?'

'Simple – "are you interested in going on a double date?"'

'Mmm … I'll do it later.'

'Okay. Anyway enough about that, how's your day been?'

'Actually, I got a call from a girl I've met at dancing. She needed someone to talk to, so I agreed to meet her.'

'Is she okay?'

'I think so,' Stephanie hesitated. 'I think she just needs a friend … although she has a major crush on the dance teacher. It's so obvious.'

Emma blew gently on the top of her spoon to cool the soup down. 'So tell me some more about this dance teacher?'

'His name is Anton … He's tall with dark brown, curly hair. I guess he looks a little bit like Andrew in some ways. And there's something about him…'

Emma's eyes widened. 'Stephanie, are you attracted to Anton? You're starting to blush.'

'I'm not sure … When I dance with him I feel so happy. I think he's sexy but I really don't know… I still miss Andrew every day …'

'I know you would, that's a normal way to feel but surely he would want you to love again.'

Stephanie's eyes began to water. Emma left her seat and placed her arm around Stephanie's shoulder.

'I'm sorry Steph. It must be hard to lose someone you love especially so early in life. I just want you to be happy.'

Stephanie shivered. 'I know. Thank you. I guess it's silly that I feel like this still. Maybe I need to move on.'

'Are you okay, Stephanie?'

'I think I just need to rest.'

'I'll clear the dishes and let myself out. You go and have a good sleep.'

'Thanks.'

Chapter Nineteen

Stephanie lay on her bed – it was still too early to sleep.

Emma had been so excited about Daniel and the double date yet Anton seemed to occupy Stephanie's thoughts. *There's just something about Anton and the way he looks at me.* She closed her eyes and pictured herself dancing ...

There she was in the centre of the dance floor dancing the Salsa steps. Swaying her hips to the spicy Latin beat she wondered where he was. Dancing had become so addictive now. A shadow was cast on the floor. Was that him? Was it Anton? Stephanie was about to turn around.

Ding dong!

'Stephanie, you have another visitor! He's sitting in the kitchen!' her mother called.

'Wayne, what a surprise ... '

'Stephanie, it's been so long since I saw you. How are you?'

'I'm okay ... ' Stephanie found herself not knowing where to look.

Wayne stared back at her. 'I miss Webbo so much. When I kick the soccer ball around I wish he was there.'

'Yeah ... I miss him too.'

'Stephanie, I need to tell you something about Andrew ...'

'What about Andrew?'

'That night … at the pub … well, I introduced Andrew to a bloke who had a snake tattoo. I met him overseas. They shared a few drinks … I think he may have had something to do with Andrew's death.'

'What!' Stephanie turned her face away from Wayne.

'Sorry, I didn't mean to upset you.'

'Just go … '

'Stephanie, I'm sorry … I really am. I just needed to tell you. You have my number if you want to call me.' Standing up from the table, he made his way to the front door.

A car hit Andrew when he left the pub, that's what she was told. It just didn't make sense. She rushed to her bedroom, leaped onto bed and lay under the covers.

Who was this man? Why was he talking to Andrew? If only I could turn back time, she thought.

Closing her eyes, she could see the scene all over again- the phone ringing … her mother answering the call … that dreaded call that informed her that Andrew was dead.

Wayne was the last person to be with Andrew. *Why did he have to tell me all this? I wish Wayne hadn't come over. I don't want him in my life anymore…*

Stephanie awoke to the sound of her bedside alarm. *Monday morning, we meet again,* she groaned internally.

Recklessly, she pulled on a pair of black pants and a white shirt. Standing in front of the mirror, she gave her hair a five second brush. *No time for break*fast, she thought.

'Bye Mum, I'm off!'

'But you haven't had anything to eat?'

'I'm not that hungry. I'll get something later.'

She grabbed her jacket and made her way out the door and into the cold air.

The train was crowded on a Monday morning with people making their way to work. She had five stops until Hampton Station. People read the newspaper, listened to music or played on their phones but Anton was on Stephanie's mind. Was he thinking about her?

The train stopped at Hampton Station and Stephanie hurried off.

'Stephanie, come and look at this,' Emma had her eyes glued to her computer screen. 'Look at this story ... there was a stabbing in Elwood, near where you live.'

Stephanie eyed the black text in front of her.

'That's only a few streets from me. How scary. I didn't think something like that would happen in Elwood.'

'Let me make you a coffee.' Emma got up from her desk.

'Thanks, that would be lovely.' Stephanie took a deep breath and looked at the pile of paper that was lying on her desk. Last time she had been at work she had not been bothered to deal with it all. On the other side of her desk was a pile of books.

'Here you go, that'll make you feel better,' Emma said placing the mug onto the desk.

'Thanks.' Stephanie picked up her mug and took a few sips.

Focus Stephanie. You're at work, get on with your job. With that thought, she picked up the book on the top of the pile and read the title – *Tropical Travel Destinations*. The cover showed a sunny beach scene. Stephanie and Andrew had planned to go to Bali some day. Andrew, being born in England, had hated the cold weather and loved the sunshine.

Ally entered through the front door and marched towards her computer.

'I really should change that poster display to promote a new novel. Steph, this letter is for you. I had Wayne knocking at the door at 8:30 this morning. I told him we were not open yet but he insisted that I give this to you. I haven't seen him in ages. Not that I'm complaining. The bank line was so long and then the queue in the post office. Seems like everyone is doing their jobs before lunch.' Ally started madly tapping on her keyboard. 'It's nice and warm in here. Stephanie, you're very quiet?'

'Emma just showed me a newspaper article about a murder in Elwood.'

Ally stopped typing. 'You live in Elwood. What happened?'

'The article was short, something about a break in during the night that then led to a murder. The article finished by mentioning that the case is still being investigated.'

'Scary stuff, Stephanie. Don't go walking around at night on your own and make sure your doors are locked.'

'I've walked down the street where that murder happened.'

Ally gasped. 'I think you should avoid that street. Elwood seems like a safe area but after hearing that news – '

'I've caught a taxi home a few times recently,' Stephanie butted in.

'You'll be fine,' Emma said. 'You're a smart girl.'

Stephanie sat back at her desk. Covering her face with her hands, she really did not want to hear anymore.

Ring ring, ring ring!

'Hello Hampton Library, Alison speaking, how may I help you?'

Emma looked over at Stephanie from across the room and rolled her eyes.

Stephanie looked at her watch. *Lunchtime!* She wondered if Eve was going to the social night. She pulled her mobile out from her bag and sent her a text.

Hey, are you going to Anton's social dance night on Saturday?

Eve replied immediately.

Yep. I need a new dress. Come late night shopping with me on Thursday night?

Stephanie texted back.

Yeah sure.

Before she had time to send the text, Ally was off the phone. 'By the way girls, we're going to close early today at 4. I've a lady from the council visiting. I hope that's okay with you.'

'Fine with me,' Emma said.

'Me too,' Stephanie answered.

Stephanie deleted the text she had typed.

Can we meet say at 4:30pm today?

Yep, I'll meet you at the Red Cross shop in Elsternwick shopping centre.

'Look at the time!' Emma exclaimed as she got up from her chair. '1:30! Time for lunch break. Do you want me to get you something, Steph?'

'If you're going to the coffee shop, can you please get me a latte?'

'Sure. And you, Ally?'

'Nothing, thanks. I've got so much work to do here.'

Chapter Twenty

Returning to her work, Stephanie stared at the computer screen.

There were so many new books to enter in the data system - Ancient Egypt, Argentina, Peru, South America - the list of travel books went on and on.

She had not got to finish reading *The Undiscovered Worlds of Peru.*

The Incas world was so different ... 'gods', 'animals', and 'sacrifice', Stephanie thought as she shivered in her chair

The door slid open and Emma walked in carrying two coffees.

'Here you go, second coffee for the day. That's what work is about!' she said with a laugh.

'Thanks, Em ... *Ahhh-CHOO!'*

A lady looked up from reading her book.

'Bless you. You're still sick? You need to drink plenty of water,' Emma whispered as she walked past.

Stephanie grabbed a tissue and wiped her runny nose as a lady with greyish hair approached.

'I'm not sure where these books go. Someone left them on the table.'

'That's fine, I'll put them away.'

As she rested her arm back on the table, she felt a wet sensation. Her eyes caught sight of her cup that was now horizontal and the brown liquid was seeping out and making its way towards the pile of books. *Damn!*

Stephanie grabbed the books and dropped them onto the floor. She reached for the soft white tissues. They started turning brown as she wiped the mess. *Back to work …*

Type, type, type, enter, type, type, type, enter. Her fingers madly pressed on the keys for the next hour.

'Look at the time.' Emma stood in front of Stephanie's desk.

Stephanie looked at her watch. Ten to four.

'Time to switch off the computers, girls,' Ally said.

'After this visit from the council, I've invited Shane to come over tonight. I want to cook dinner for him. I was thinking of making him a pasta dish since I'm not the best cook, but on second thoughts, maybe that's not a good idea. I'm not sure if he really likes Italian food. What do you think, girls?'

'Stick with a good old roast and vegetables, Alison. That's a safe bet.'

'What do you think, Stephanie?'

'I think you need to be yourself. If you want to cook pasta, just do that.'

Ally grabbed her bag and made her way to the office. 'Thanks, Steph' she said in a sarcastic voice.

Flicking the off button on her computer screen Stephanie reached for the letter from Wayne and stuffed it into her pocket.

The two girls grabbed their bags and made their way out the electronic doors.

'Take care, Steph' Emma hugged her as they parted company.

'You too, Em.'

'Call me if you need to.'

Stephanie approached the train station as the boom gate started to come down across the road. *Damn ... missed the train,* she thought.

The cars rushed past as the gates opened. A little girl and her mother passed her. The two females were holding hands and were laughing. Stephanie had forgotten what it was like to have a good laugh.

Walking along the beach with Andrew on that last day was a vision she still had daily, snuggling into his muscular body. Andrew was so fit and healthy. If Wayne had not crossed their path that day, would Andrew still be alive?

Reaching the platform, she made her way to the wooden bench and leaned her back against the brick wall.

She searched in her pocket for a tissue but instead ended up pulling out Wayne's note. Stephanie tore open the envelope, wondering what it was all about. A tiny yellow square post-it-note was inside. On it, there were some words written in black ink.

Stephanie, I found this on the Internet. It mentions a guy with a snake tattoo who targets sports people. I thought it might interest you. Wayne.

Stephanie heard the train coming and put the yellow note in her pocket but held onto the white paper.

The doors of the train opened and Stephanie made her way to a seat on the left side. She started looking at the piece of paper.

The black text jumped off the white page.

SOUTH AMERICAN CRIMINALS – BROTHERS ON THE LOOSE AND HEADED TO AUSTRALIA

South America's most wanted criminals have fled the country and have taken up residence in Australia. Their exact location is still unknown.

Australia has become a prime target due to our soaring drug use and high prices on the streets.

The brothers known for drug dealing grew up in Peru. Being involved in the underworld and witnessing violence during their upbringing, they dispose of their victims in brutal ways.

A Melbourne businesswoman was murdered in what is believed to be a revenge attack over money. Her battered body was left in the boot of a car outside a pub where she may have taken hours to die. The case is still being investigated.

The South American brothers are considered suspects. They have established contacts with organised crime cells here, including Asian gangs and bikies. They seem to target sports people, entertainers and young women.

The two brothers are tall, dark-haired men. One brother can be identified by a snake tattoo.

Since 2012, Peru has been the world's top producer of esctasy. The prices in Australia makes it a good market.

Last week, Peruvian police arrested six Peruvians and two Mexicans as authorities found ecstasy at a dance party also known as a rave party. Ecstasy commonly called 'The love drug' can raise the body temperature to dangerous levels. It is one of a growing number of 'designer drugs.' Police questioned whether this could possibly be another operation the brothers are involved in.

The following week a rural home was raided and more ecstasy found. A further four people were arrested by Police all suspected to be linked to this case.

An Australian Federal Police spokeswoman said South American syndicates would continue to look at Australia as they feel the expense is worth it because of the high prices they can obtain.

Stephanie sighed. Why had Wayne given her this article? He had come to her house last night talking about some guy with a snake tattoo… A lot of people had tattoos these days, especially of animals. Stephanie's uncle Gary had an anchor tattoo as he had been in the navy and his best mate had one of a crow.

Stephanie stuffed the paper back into her pocket as the train stopped at Elsternwick Station. Examining her watch, she knew she had roughly fifteen minutes until she had to meet Eve.

Chapter Twenty-One

'Let's go in!' ordered Eve as soon as Stephanie arrived.

The two girls entered the shop. A sea of bright clothes hung on racks. Eve strolled over to a rack that had several dresses. Stephanie pinched her nose. *Phew!* A girl with pink spiky hair and a silver stud in her nose was searching through the rack next to her.

'What do you think of this dress?' Eve held up a short red velvet dress with shoestring straps. 'I want to wear a dress to the dance night. Where's the mirror?'

'I think I saw it over there.'

Eve rushed over and admired herself in the tiny mirror.

'I like the dress but I need to get rid of these glasses. I'm going to get some contact lenses.'

'The dress looks really nice. Red suits you Eve.'

Eve did a little twirl and then started to stroll back and forth pretending she was in a fashion parade.

A smile appeared on her face. 'I want to look sexy for Anton. I was thinking of painting my nails red too.'

Stephanie looked down at her chewed fingernails. She hardly ever painted them.

'I think this is the one I'm going to buy. That was easy, no more looking.' She grabbed the tag. 'Ten dollars, that's a reasonable price.' Pulling out her wallet, she checked to see if she had the right money. 'Just enough! I was a bit worried. Actually I think I may need a necklace too. I'll just use dad's credit card to pay for it.'

Stephanie followed close behind Eve, as she wandered over to a glass cabinet.

'Do you like that one, Steph?'

'Yeah, try it on.'

Eve frowned and turned her back.

Stephanie stared into the glass cabinet looking at the variety of rings and necklaces.

A lady suddenly pushed past her with her young son.

'This jumper will have to do.'

'Muuuum! I don't like it.'

'Too bad, you have to do what you're told!' the lady snapped before taking a quick glance around the store. She grabbed a silk scarf that was hanging on the rack and handed it to her son. 'Put this in your jacket pocket.' Dropping the jumper on the floor, she clutched the boy's hand and left the shop.

Stephanie's jaw dropped. She could not believe what she had just witnessed. Looking around for Eve, she spotted her standing at the front counter.

'What a great find.'

'I know, right!' boasted Eve.

'Sorry to interrupt but I think the lady who was just in the shop with her son stole one of your scarves.'

The girl pulled a face. 'I'm not surprised, it happens all the time. We don't even bother to report it anymore. Thanks for letting us know though.'

Stephanie wrinkled her nose. Stealing did not sit well with her at all...

'Shall we get a coffee?' Eve suggested.

'Yeah, why not.'

'Let's just go to the place across the road.'

'I'm so happy I got a new dress. I hope Anton will like it. Red is my colour – '

'Can I take your order?' the waiter interrupted.

'A skinny latte, please.'

'And you?'

'A hot chocolate.'

'Anything else?'

'No thanks.'

'I wonder what Helena will wear? That will be interesting.'

'Who knows,' Stephanie gazed out the window.

'Are you listening to me?'

'Sorry Eve, I must be daydreaming. What were we talking about?' Stephanie muttered. 'Dresses?'

Eve frowned. 'What are you going to wear?'

'Not sure yet, haven't really thought about it.'

'As if!'

Stephanie shrugged.

'Hmmm. Anyway, so, I've never asked, do you have a boyfriend?'

'Your drinks, ladies,' the waiter chimed, returning to the table.

'Thank you.'

'So … do you have a boyfriend?' Eve repeated.

'I did … but not anymore.'

Eve started to drink her hot chocolate while Stephanie continued to stare out the window.

'I've never had a boyfriend,' Eve continued. 'So … what do

you think I should talk to Anton about?'

Stephanie took another sip of her coffee. 'Well, we know he likes dancing.'

'BORING! He does that all the time … '

'True … '

'What else can I talk to him about?' Eve asked.

'Just make general chit chat about yourself.'

'What if he doesn't like me? This happens all the time! Story of my life … '

'Every situation is different, Eve,' reassured Stephanie.

Eve bit her lip as the two girls sat in an awkward silence for a few moments.

'Well, I'm off … Thanks for shopping with me,' Eve said abruptly. 'Oh and can you pay? I'll pay next time.'

'Yeah … bye?' Stephanie called out. She paid for the two drinks and left.

Far out … what a day, she thought as she searched for Lance's business card in her bag.

'Yellow Transport Taxis, Lance speaking.'

'Hi Lance, it's Stephanie.'

'I thought I recognised the voice.'

'I'm in Elsternwick shopping centre.'

'That's lucky, I'm in Caulfield and I don't have a fare at the moment. Want me to pick you up?'

'That would be great.'

'Pick you up outside the ice cream shop on Glenhuntly Road.'

'Thanks. See you soon.'

Stephanie waited patiently outside the ice cream shop. Next door to the shop was a small toy store. Less than a year ago, she had been there with Andrew to buy a present for her cousin.

The soft cuddly brown bear had a red ribbon tied around its neck. The bear had been sitting in the front window when Stephanie had spotted it. Andrew had thought the bear was the perfect gift. *Gee, I wish you were here, Andrew,* she thought. *Life is not fair!*

HONK!

Stephanie jumped.

A car was roaring down the main street. She shook her head in disgust. People were so impatient these days.

Next a yellow taxi pulled up at the side of the road.

'Stephanie!' a voice called from the car window.

Walking over to the car, she opened the back door and got in.

'To Elwood?' Lance asked.

'Yes please. Been busy?'

'I had a few fares. One lady I drove to the airport. She was heading to America and Mrs Lacy, took her to do grocery shopping and a few others. But the best news of the day is I heard on the radio that tickets for *Dirty Dancing* are being released.'

'Really! I didn't know the show was coming to Melbourne. Do you like the theatre?'

'Ha! You wouldn't think I like that stuff … but my mother was an actress so I used to go watch her in all the shows … So yeah, to answer your question, I do like the theatre.'

'And now what does she do?'

'She spends her time looking after my brother's kids … Oh, do you like this song?' Lance turned up the volume.

'It has a good beat. Reminds me of some of the music we dance to.'

'Cool … Have you seen the video clip for it?'

'I think so …'

'A girl running in the rain.'

'Yes I know the one,' Stephanie said with a giggle.

'Then a good looking guy stops her in the street,' Lance laughed. 'My friend said I look like the guy.'

Stephanie took a side-glance. 'Guess you both have short blonde hair.'

'I know one difference – I can't sing like him.' Lance admitted. 'Anyway, how has your day been?'

'I worked at the library and then met a friend. She needed to buy a dress for our dance function. It's on Saturday.'

'Saturday! Not long.'

'Since you like theatre, did you want to come?' The words had just come out of Stephanie's mouth without thinking.

Lance scratched his head, looking into his rear vision mirror. 'The thing is … I can't dance.'

'That doesn't matter.'

'Hmm, should really broaden my horizon, right?'

'Right,' Stephanie agreed.

'Count me in.'

The taxi arrived at Stephanie's place.

She handed over the money and then searched for the details saved in her phone.

'The dance function is at Rendezvous Restaurant, 400 Church Street, Richmond. It starts at 8:30 with a $20 entry fee.'

'I'll try to make it, Stephanie. Thanks.'

'No worries, Lance.'

Had she just invited a stranger to the dance function? Weirdly, Stephanie felt a connection to Lance, despite having met him only a few times. *He's warm, friendly and, well, quite easy on the eye,* Stephanie thought to herself. *Why not invite him?*

As she walked towards to her front door, she felt somewhat proud of her spontaneous behaviour.

Chapter Twenty-Two

Exhausted, Stephanie flopped onto the couch and turned on the TV.

In an attempt to warm her near-frozen limbs, she threw a knitted blanket over her legs and placed her icy hands in her pockets. Touching some paper, she remembered Wayne's note. *Hmmm, better call him I guess - not that I want talk to him …*

Scrolling through her phone, she found Wayne's number and hit call. She waited - no answer. Just as she was about to hang up, Wayne picked up.

'Steph … hey.'

'Hey … '

For a minute there was silence on the other end of the phone.

'So I guess you got my note? '

'Yeah … I just wanted to ask you more about it.'

Wayne breathed heavily into the phone. 'I don't want to talk to you about it over the phone. Can we meet for dinner tomorrow night and discuss it then?'

'I guess so…'

'I'll meet you tomorrow night at the Japanese place across the road from the train station in Hampton Street at 6,' Wayne mumbled into the phone. 'See you then.' With that, he hung up.

Stephanie started to grind her teeth. *What am I doing? I don't want to meet Wayne alone,* she thought. Still holding her mobile, she rang Emma.

'Hey Steph!'

'Hey Em …'

'What's up?'

'So … I was just speaking to Wayne.'

'Wayne? Why were you talking to him?'

'Well, he left a note for me with Ally. Maybe something linked to Andrew's death. He seems to think there was more to it.'

'Serious?' Emma inquired.

'I'll explain later. I was actually ringing you because I need your support.'

'How can I help?'

'Wayne wants me to meet him for dinner tomorrow night.'

'Tomorrow night?'

'Yeah, in Hampton Street after work. I don't want to go alone. Will you come with me?'

'Of course I will.'

Stephanie breathed a sigh of relief. 'Thanks so much, Emma.'

'No problem, Steph. Oh my god, just off the topic, I'm chatting to Oliver, he's so sweet! He's addicted to chocolate like me. Oh and he's agreed to the double date so you have to ask Daniel.'

'Should I?'

'Of course! Hang on, Oliver just sent another message. Sorry Steph, I've gotta go. Message Daniel now. I'll see you at work tomorrow.'

'But what do I say?'

'Lygon Street, Italian restaurant, double date. I'm off, bye!'

Stephanie hit the Flirtnow app and followed Emma's

instructions. She did not wait for a reply. Breathing a sigh of relief she was glad Emma had agreed to being her companion when meeting Wayne.

The front door opened.

'We're home, darling!' her mother called out as she walked towards Stephanie. 'Fancy watching television with your father and I?'

'No thanks. I'm going to my room.'

'Is everything alright?'

'Just another busy day.'

'I'm here to talk if you need to?' her mother reassured.

'Everything is fine, Mum. But thank you.'

'Okay. Just checking, darling.'

Stephanie's bedroom was her safe place and the idea of being in her pyjamas was comforting. She went to close her curtain to see a black cat was outside. How she wished she could bring him inside but knew her parents would not approve. She tiptoed back into the kitchen and put some milk in a bowl. Not wanting to get caught she quickly left the bowl outside the back door.

'Is everything alright?' her mother called out.

'I'm fine! Just getting a glass of water.'

When she returned to her room, the cat had disappeared. Stephanie rested on the bed.

Switching off her bedside lamp she gently shut her eyes.

Her phone began to ring. Eve calling.

'Hello?'

'Did I wake you?'

'No, I was just relaxing.'

'I'm glad I got home when I did. Just made it in time before Dad arrived,' Eve groaned. 'He has a new lady. She makes me sick. Covered in tattoos and she has a stud in her nose. I better whisper, I don't want them to hear me.'

Stephanie sat up in her bed as she continued to listen.

'The two of them are drinking in the front room. I don't want to leave my room. I needed someone to talk to.'

'Are you okay?' Stephanie asked.

'I'm fine. I just don't want to go out there. Maybe I should climb out the window and run away … but where would I go?'

'Don't do that ' Stephanie muttered.

'Why not?' Eve groaned. 'You don't know what my life is like. You don't understand. This is not helping me talking to you. Thanks for nothing, Steph.'

'Eve, wait – ' Stephanie had no time to respond, Eve had hung up. Stephanie decided to text her.

Sorry Eve, I'm here to talk. Take care and see you at dancing. S x

Thanks. E x

Stephanie sighed, she hoped Eve was okay but there was nothing much she could do.

Stephanie sat at her desk rubbing her eyes - she hadn't got much sleep last night.

It was only 9 o'clock but there were already so many people in the library. Stephanie watched Ally handling all the inquiries as people stood at the front desk. Switching on her computer she began to enter a book into the catalogue, *My Country* by Paul Gonman.

'Excuse me, dear. Would you please direct me to the non-fiction section?'

'Just over to your left, towards the back of the library.'

'Thank you.'

Emma stood at the desk holding a pile of books.

'Has he replied about the date yet?'

'I've not checked.'

'Steph ... look in your break.'

'Okay.'

'Guess what I did this morning? A crossword. There was only one I couldn't work out. I may ask you later. I've so many books to re-shelf, this job is going to take me a while.'

Stephanie stared back at her computer screen. She needed to enter the next book, *Mr. Wrong* by John Fareside. As her fingers madly tapped on the keyboard, she accidentally hit a wrong button, causing Google to appear on the screen.

Might as well have a little break, Stephanie thought as she stared at the Google search bar. She typed the word 'criminals' and hit the search button. She wanted to do some research before she saw Wayne. The first result that appeared was Wikipedia. Stephanie clicked on the link. Her eyes darted across the page. She moved closer towards the screen and read on.

Criminal offence may involve not only hurting an individual but also a community. Theft, rape and murder are all criminal acts.

She scrolled to the end of the page where many words were listed. 'Crime', 'offence', 'law breaking', 'criminals', 'drug dealing', the list went on and on.

'Drug dealing', were the words she clicked on next. A list appeared at the top of the page:

What makes a good drug dealer?

- Good connections.
- Always have money put away for bail.
- A love of the game.
- Never let your guard down.
- Good supplies.
- A sweet dealing nickname will help.
- You should have a gun or a knife.

Remember, you are in it for the money and nothing else.

Stephanie gasped when she read the last line. She quickly clicked on the cross at the corner of the computer screen.

'Andrew, come here,' a girl called out to a young guy with a toned body. 'I need to find a book on muscle groups for my university assignment.'

'Sure, Kelly. I'll help you look.'

For a split second Stephanie had thought Andrew was back.

'Are you okay, Stephanie?' Emma had returned.

'I just heard someone calling the name Andrew and for a minute I thought he was back.'

'Stephanie, so many guys are called Andrew. Anyway, I want to ask you about the crossword. Five letters down, the clue is South American people from an ancient civilization. South America is a place I don't know a lot about. It starts with the letter I,' Emma inquired.

'I think I know the answer,' Stephanie paused. 'Is it Incas? Does that fit?'

'How do you spell it?'

Stephanie sighed, 'I think it is I. N. C. A. S.'

'Yes, that fits. How did you know the answer?'

'I've been looking at a book recently about South America.'

'That sounds cool.'

Stephanie nodded. 'It's pretty interesting. South America is a place I would like to visit some day.'

Emma interrupted. 'What's the title of the book?'

'*The Undiscovered Worlds of Peru.*'

'I haven't seen that book. What does it look like?' Emma sat at her desk.

'It has a dark cover with gold writing. You should borrow it when I've finished.'

'I will,' Emma said with a smile.

'I'm finding the part on the Inca culture fascinating. There was so much symbolism in their world.'

'Symbolism, you already have me interested.' Emma sat back in her seat. 'Go on ... tell me some more.'

'Well, animals represented their three different worlds, being the World of the Gods, the World of the Living and the World of the Dead.'

'World of the Dead?' Emma was shocked.

'Yes, World of the Dead.'

'What animal represented the World of the Dead? Let me guess... a vulture?'

'Interesting answer,' Stephanie replied. 'Birds represented the World of the Gods. A snake represented the World of the Dead.' Stephanie could not believe she had remembered so much about the book.

'I should have guessed the snake. So what animal represented the World of the Living? A horse?'

'No,' Stephanie chuckled. 'A cat.'

'I think cats were sacred in ancient Egyptian society. I must borrow a book on Egypt again. They were fascinating people too, who believed in gods. Why are you reading *The Undiscovered*

Worlds of Peru?' Emma was curious.

'A lady returned the book and told me she had found it interesting. It was as if I was meant to read it. I would never have just picked it up off the shelf. But there was one part I didn't like … '

'What was that?'

'The part about the Incas believing strongly in sacrifice.'

'Sacrifice!'

'Sacrifice in giving back to the Gods.'

'I have to read this book, Steph. Make sure you give it to me when you're finished'

'Yeah, I will.'

Emma looked at her watch. 'Oh, nearly time to meet Wayne. Are you ready?'

Stephanie bit her lip.

'I guess so.'

'Let's get going.'

Chapter Twenty-Three

'I wonder what this is all about?'

'We'll find out soon.'

An 'open' sign hung from the red door of the Japanese restaurant. Stephanie and Emma entered.

'Table for two?'

'Three people, please.'

'Of course, follow me.'

The smell of chicken cooking wafted in the air as they past the open kitchen window.

Emma sat in the wooden chair opposite Stephanie. The waitress placed a black folder in front of them.

'I'll leave you the menu to look at.'

Emma studied the menu in front of her. 'Misu soup, teriyaki chicken, I don't know what to choose.'

Stephanie looked out the window. *Where is he?* she wondered.

She could hear the sound of the train as it passed through the railway crossing. The red lights were flashing and people were standing at the boom gates waiting patiently to cross. Watching the boom gates rise, she saw a man approaching the Japanese restaurant.

A guy in a long, dark coat walked up to their table. It was Wayne.

'Stephanie, I thought you were coming alone?'

'Sorry Wayne, this is Emma. She works with me at the library.'

'Hi, I think we may have met before,' Emma said as she held out her hand.

Wayne ignored her comment and sat in the empty chair.

'Steph … What I say does not leave this table, get it?' Wayne said sternly.

Stephanie nodded.

Emma looked back at her menu. 'Just need to go to the bathroom, back in a second.'

Wayne began to whisper. 'Stephanie, I've never told you this but … I've taken drugs … ecstasy, actually.' His eyes darted around the room.

Stephanie's jaw dropped. 'How did you get it?'

'Remember when I went to Barcelona for a holiday and to watch the soccer?'

'Yes, vaguely.'

'Well, when I was in Barcelona, I made friends with a guy who was a drug dealer …' Wayne glanced over at the other tables for a minute. 'I just want to make sure no one is listening,' he muttered.

'Continue … ' Stephanie replied.

'So, we'd go party on the waterfront till all hours of the morning. One night he found out that I played soccer – '

'Wayne, I'm confused,' Stephanie interrupted.

Wayne crossed his arms and continued to talk. 'He said he'd met loads of soccer players and loved to help them. Then, a few days later, he introduced me to drugs.'

Stephanie huffed. 'That's not my business to judge you, Wayne.'

'I'm going to make my point. Hear me out! This guy and I stayed in touch and he said some day he might visit Australia. I didn't hear from him for a while and then one day he called.'

'Sorry Wayne, but I just don't get what this has to do with Andrew?'

Wayne sighed. 'I'm getting to that. So he was in Melbourne and wanted to meet up.'

'He was in Melbourne?'

'Yeah ... and the night I met up with him was the night of Andrew's death.'

Stephanie gasped. 'This drug dealer was there on the night of his death?'

'I'm afraid so ... and I introduced Andrew to the guy with the snake tattoo.' Wayne looked down at the ground. 'I feel guilty. I tried so many times to convince Andrew to take drugs.'

'Andrew never told me that.'

'I know, he was upset that he didn't win the Best and Fairest award. I wanted to help him feel better again. I know the drug helped me.' Wayne took a deep breath and looked back at Stephanie. 'I never wanted him to die.'

Stephanie's eyes began to water, she did not know if she wanted to hear anymore.

Wayne grabbed Stephanie's hand. His hand was trembling.

'Stephanie ...' he whispered. 'The guy with the snake tattoo gave Andrew drugs.'

She gasped. 'But Wayne, he was hit by a car?'

'Stephanie, I was there. I know what happened. I just couldn't tell you until now. I needed time.'

'You needed time!' Stephanie clenched her fist.

'Please, let me finish. I was on the Internet the other day and found that article. The words "drug dealers" and "snake tattoo" rang in my ears. Stephanie, I've not touched drugs since. I loved Webbo. Andrew was my best friend.'

Stephanie sighed. 'I can't believe you are telling me this now.'

'You have to understand, I couldn't tell the police,' Wayne grumbled. 'I could have been in trouble. They may have put me in jail.'

Stephanie let go of Wayne's hand, took off her jacket and put it on the back of her chair.

'Are you okay?' Emma had returned to the table. 'You look hot. Do you need some water to drink?'

'Yes please,' Stephanie answered trying to fight back tears.

Emma left the table, got some water from the counter and returned to her seat.

Stephanie held the glass in her hot hands. The cool water trickled down her throat. As she placed the glass onto the wooden table, she took a deep breath.

'I know it's a lot to take in… but I had to tell you… I felt I owed it to Andrew,' Wayne continued.

'Can I take your order?' The waitress interrupted.

'I'll have Miso soup, Gyoza and the Teriyaki Chicken Don.' Emma handed her the menu.

'And you, miss?'

'I'll have the Teriyaki Chicken Don.'

'Is that all, miss?'

'Yes, thank you.'

'And you, sir?'

'Nothing, thanks. Stephanie, I'm going to make tracks. You have my number. Call me if you need to.'

Standing up from the table and turning his collar up around his neck, Wayne made his way out of the restaurant, down the street and across the railway line.

'So one Miso soup, one Gyoza, two Teriyaki Chicken Don?'

'Yep, that's it.'

'Did you find out any more information?' Emma whispered across the table.

'I think I better not talk about it here,' Stephanie's eyes darted around the room, a young couple were holding hands across the table opposite them.

'I don't think they would care what we're saying,' Emma said.

'But better be on the safe side. I just want to say one thing ... whatever you do, please be careful. You're my best friend and I don't want anything to happen to you.'

'Miso soup, Gyoza and the two Teriyaki Chicken Dons, enjoy,' the waiter said as she placed the dishes in front of them.

The steam rose from the cloudy liquid. 'Is that seaweed in my soup?'

'Yes, Emma. Miso soup has seaweed in it.'

'Doesn't taste bad, I could get used to this,' Emma said taking a mouthful.

They watched people walk past as they ate their meals.

'So many people catch the train these days.'

Stephanie sighed. 'I catch the train to work and dancing.'

'How is the dancing going?'

'Well, I love dancing but I'm still learning the Latin steps. There's so much hip movement involved.'

Emma raised her eyebrows. 'I couldn't dance to save myself. Have you spoken to your dance teacher again?'

Stephanie began to choke.

'Have some water,' Emma handed her the glass.

'Some rice got stuck in my throat.'

'Don't talk, just keep drinking. I'm glad that Wayne's gone. There's something about him that I don't like,' Emma said before finishing the last mouthful of her food.

Stephanie took a deep breath. 'Everything is such a mystery. When I visited Madam Farrell she knew I had come to her for answers but at the end of the session I was still confused.'

'Can I ask … what did she say?'

'Well, when she looked into her crystal ball she could see a man in my life who was tall and attractive. I immediately thought of Andrew but she said it was a man who was going to enter my life.'

'How strange … '

'The story gets more interesting. Apparently, this man is going to have a big influence.'

'Good or bad?' Emma asked.

'Not sure. Then she went onto talking about the beach. The beach was the last place I was with Andrew. I'm so confused, Emma…'

'Let's leave and talk somewhere else. I'll get this one Steph.' She left the table and made her way to the counter.

Chapter Twenty-Four

'Damn,' Emma mumbled as she rummaged through her her bag.

'What's wrong?' Stephanie asked.

'I think I left my phone charger at work. I need it. Can we go back?'

'Yeah, sure.'

The two girls made their way down the empty street towards the library.

'Look at the moon.' Emma commented. 'It's so bright tonight!'

'The last time I saw Madam Farrell she said there was a full moon recently. She said her cat acts strangely when there's a full moon.'

Emma's eyes widened. 'You need to tell me more about Madam Farrell.'

'It was interesting going to see her,' Stephanie said.

'I was actually thinking of going and asking her about Oliver and my love life. What do you think?'

'Mmm … maybe.'

'On second thoughts, maybe I'll wait till after the double date. Anyway, so what happened, tell me more?'

Stephanie shrugged. 'Well, when I arrived I sat in her room and there was a crystal ball on the table. I had to close my eyes. She also told me about a bird, tall dark figure and the full moon. Seeing the moon tonight reminded me of her.'

'Sounds like she saw lots of interesting – '

'She also mentioned a cat and snake,' Stephanie interrupted. 'Nothing makes sense...'

'How did it end?'

'She saw a word in the crystal ball.'

'What did it say?'

'Sacrifice,' Stephanie whispered.

Emma gasped. 'Sacrifice?'

Stephanie nodded.

'That's scary. I wonder what she meant.'

The two girls arrived outside the library.

Emma turned to Stephanie. 'Sacrifice … you said the Incas believed strongly in sacrifice.'

Stephanie frowned. She thought that was a strange thing for Emma to say.

'Don't look at me like that. I have Incas on the brain now you mentioned that book. It's also weird that Madam Farrell spoke about a bird, cat and snake,' Emma mumbled. 'You said the Incas associated animals with different worlds.'

Stephanie nodded. 'Maybe that's what the reading was relating to, the book on Peru.'

'So, what did Wayne say … '

'He mentioned drug dealing. Some guy he reckons with a snake tattoo gave Andrew drugs on the night he was hit by the car.'

'Drug dealing … Oh shit … '

'You know Wayne left me a letter with Ally at work … In it was an article about drug dealers.' Stephanie said.

'You know what, I'm going to have a quick look on the

Internet when we go inside,' Emma suggested.

She pushed the button to activate the door and the two girls walked in.

'I'm not going to turn on the main light. I don't want people to know we're here. Come and share my computer.'

The computer screen lit the room.

'So I'm thinking of searching for – '

'Type "criminals", "snake tattoo", and see what comes up,' Stephanie advised. 'That's what Wayne's article mentioned.' Stephanie closed her eyes for just a second. She hoped that Emma would find some answers.

'Mmm, interesting.'

Stephanie opened her eyes again to see Emma clicking on a link.

'"Criminal brothers, are drugs still on their minds? Main trafficker can be identified by a snake tattoo." Steph, look … '

Drug dealing in Australia over the last year has increased. It is believed overseas dealers have touched our shores and have broken into the market. Highly successful brothers, dealers from Peru, are alleged to be operating locally targeting sportsmen. The main dealer has a snake tattoo. South American authorities have been trying to track these criminals for years and bring them to justice. If you have any further information please contact Victoria Police on the number below …

Stephanie gasped. 'This article sounds similar to the one Wayne gave me. They both mention brothers from Peru who are involved in drug dealing and – '

'So Andrew took drugs?'

'Emma, please stop … ' A tear ran down Stephanie's cheek.

'But these guys could be responsible!' Emma said outraged.

'I'm not sure about that. Wayne only mentioned one drug dealer. Please Emma, no more tonight, I need some time to think.'

Emma placed her arm around Stephanie. 'I just wanted to help you. We may be able to find some answers.'

'I want to visit Andrew's grave,' Stephanie said.

'Steph … are you sure?'

'I haven't been there. I guess I wasn't ready to visit. But I want to now. Will you come with me?'

'Sure, let's go tomorrow. I'll pick you up first thing in the morning.'

The next morning Stephanie and Emma found themselves in the gardens of the crematorium and walking along the uneven path.

'The man at the front desk said to follow this path and then turn into the rose garden,' said Stephanie.

'We've been walking for a while and I can't see any roses. We must be getting close,' Emma commented.

'I'm sure the rose garden is at the back of the cemetery.'

'They need a map of this place,' Emma muttered.

Stephanie did not answer. She had only one thing on her mind and that was to go to Andrew's grave.

'Finally!' Emma came to a stop and pointed to a sign. 'Rose garden, this way.'

Stephanie smiled as she realised she would be there soon. 'Wait … '

'What's the matter?'

'Can you wait for me here? I want to go alone.'

Emma sighed. 'Okay, I'll just go sit under that gum tree and wait for you.'

Stephanie did not respond. She remained focused. The sweet fragrance of the roses surrounded her. Colours of orange, pink, red and yellow came into view. A red rose bush marked Andrew's grave.

Stephanie stood at the rose bush, her eyes fixed on Andrew's plaque. She wanted to be close to him. Bending over, her hand touched the soft, freshly mown grass. The sweet sound of chirping birds echoed in her ears. The gentle breeze blew strands of her hair that had escaped from the elastic band that held her ponytail in place. Staring at the metal plaque in front of her, she read the words out aloud.

'In memory of Andrew John Webb. Son of Patricia and Luke. In our hearts forever. Rest in Peace.'

She placed her hand over her heart. Closing her eyes, she visualised an image of Andrew in her mind. His brown eyes sparkled and he had a grin from ear to ear. In her mind, she could hear his words.

'I'm happy, Steph. Please don't worry about me. I want you to love life and be happy. I want you to find love again. I know you won't forget me. I will live in your heart forever. Do not live in the past, live for today ...'

The words were so clear it was as if Andrew was standing beside her. The wind blew stronger as she wrapped her coat closer to her chest.

'So, what should I do? Should I find out more about these drug dealers and the man with the snake tattoo?' she muttered aloud.

'No ...'

'Why not?'

'Don't go down that path, Steph. We need to let it go ...'

Stephanie opened her eyes. She glanced at the other rose bushes. The deep red flowers reminded her of Valentine's Day. Every year since Andrew and Stephanie had been dating, he had given her a red rose on Valentine's Day.

'Giving you a red rose shows my love for you, Stephanie. When you are surrounded by red roses you are surrounded by love … '

She lay on the grass and watched the white fluffy clouds above her. It's time, she told herself. Time to accept what has happened and move on. A red rose lay on the grass near her. Reaching out to pick up the stem, she admired the flower's delicate petals. They were beginning to droop. How precious life was.

Stephanie knew it was time to leave. She pushed herself up off the ground and standing on her two feet again, one by one, she picked the velvety petals from the rose and dropped them onto Andrew's grave. Carried gently by the wind, the petals landed one by one on the ground.

'Thank you,' she said.

With those final words she made her way back down the path and left the cemetery with Emma.

Chapter Twenty-Five

The cars sped past on the highway. Stephanie looked in the side mirror as she watched a black jeep that was only inches away from the back of Emma's car.

HONK!

'Move, you big bully!' Emma shouted.

The black jeep roared past them.

Emma rolled her eyes. 'People and their jeeps, he must have a big ego. Did you see him shaking his fist as he drove past me?'

Stephanie looked over at Emma. 'There are so many bullies. They drive like crazy maniacs. You never know who's driving behind the wheel.' Stephanie sighed. 'It makes me so angry that someone hit Andrew.'

'Careless drivers, let's not let them wreck our day. Anyway, to some better news – '

'Better news?' Stephanie raised an eyebrow.

'Don't look at me like that. I don't like it when you pull that face, Stephanie.'

'Sorry, I didn't mean to.'

'Don't stress, I'm just kidding. I knew you wouldn't want me to do this ... ' Emma hesitated and took a deep breath. 'I asked Ally if you could have the day off. I said I would do an extra shift for you.'

'Emma,' Stephanie said in a more relaxed voice. 'Thank you so much but you didn't have to do that.'

'I wanted to. She doesn't know everything you've been going through. I mean you haven't even had a chance to go back to the doctor, have you?'

'Emma, you're such a great friend. I wish there were more people like you in this world.'

'I just want things to get better for you,' she smiled. 'What are you going to do for the rest of the day?'

'I'm feeling a bit better after going to visit the grave. I think I may go to visit the doctor and get that check-up. I probably really should.'

'Mmm, I think that would be a good idea. Give him a call now and I can drive you there?'

'Thanks, Emma.' Stephanie reached into her bag for her phone. She scrolled through her contacts to Dr. Randle and hit call.

'Hello, it's Stephanie Walker, I was wondering if I could see Dr. Randle today?'

'There's a cancellation, would you be able to get here in half an hour's time?' said the voice on the other end.

'Yes, thank you.' Stephanie hung up her mobile. 'How lucky. They had a cancellation so I can go now.'

The car pulled up in front of Dr. Randle's clinic.

'I don't think I'll be able to stay.'

'That's okay. Thanks for everything.' She smiled at Emma and closed the car door.

Stephanie entered the sliding doors and joined the queue at the front desk. The chubby man in front of her began coughing.

'Stand still,' the lady behind her was telling her son.

'Mum, how much longer do we have to wait?'

'I'm not sure, Darren. There are three people in front of us.'

Stephanie's eyes met with a lady wearing glasses.

'Hello, how may I help you?'

'Hi, I'm Stephanie. I'm here to see Dr. Randle. I just rang a short time ago.'

'Oh yes, please take a seat.'

The leather rubbed against Stephanie's legs as she relaxed back into the chair. Stephanie discreetly pinched her nose as the smell of Dettol wafted in the air. A lady in white holding bandages walked past. The phone was continually ringing and constant chatter filled the stuffy room. The man next to her let out a loud sneeze as he reached over for a tissue.

'Thank you, Dr. Droves.'

The voice sounded familiar. Stephanie looked up to see Helena exiting a doctor's office.

'Stephanie!' Helena called out as she walked over to her. 'Fancy seeing you here.'

'Helena, how are you?'

'I'm well thanks. This is Gracie.'

'Hi Gracie.'

'She has a sore throat and we needed to get it checked.'

'She okay?' Stephanie asked.

'The doctor's put her on some medication so hopefully she'll feel better soon. How are you enjoying the dance classes?'

'Yeah, I'm loving it. I think it's the best exercise. Does Gracie dance?'

A frown appeared on Helena's face. She grabbed Gracie's hand. 'We should go for coffee sometime Stephanie ... We have to go ... can't talk now.'

Stephanie watched the two females exit through the door. *What did I say wrong?* she thought.

'Stephanie?' Dr. Randle was calling her name. 'Please come through.'

She made her way into his consulting room and sat in front of a wooden desk. Crossing her right leg over her left she tried to sit up straight.

'Last time I saw you was in the hospital.' Dr. Randle looked her right in the eyes.

'That's correct.'

'So how are you feeling now?'

'Better … ' Stephanie broke eye contact.

'You still look quite pale …' He looked down at his notes and began to scribble something on his page.

Stephanie scratched at her arm.

'Mmm, let me check something on the computer.' Swivelling on his chair, Dr. Randle started to tap on the keyboard. 'Have you been eating more now?'

'Yes, I have.'

'So you have a better appetite?'

Stephanie took a deep breath. 'Yes, I've been eating well.' Her hands trembled slightly.

'Okay, a few other questions, have you been going out much?'

'I've started Latin dancing.'

'Good! I hope you haven't been over exerting yourself?'

'Oh no. I'm taking it easy.'

Dr. Randle nodded. 'That's good to hear. Latin dancing is a great way to socialise. Just remember not to overdo it.' Dr. Randle glanced back at the computer screen. 'I see you just rang today, is there anything you needed to ask me?'

'I feel a bit better but just wanted a check-up.'

'I'll just take your blood pressure.'

The room was silent for a while as Dr. Randle carried out his work. The cuff tightened around her arm.

'Yes, everything is normal. See how you go over the next few weeks. Then you may want to come and visit me again.'

'Thank you.'

The once crowded waiting room only had a few people now sitting in it.

'I just saw Dr. Randle,' Stephanie informed the receptionist.

'Please sign and date this form. Do you need another appointment?'

'No thank you.' Stephanie handed back the pen.

'Thank you, Stephanie. Have a nice day.'

Stephanie could feel her phone vibrating in her bag. New message from Eve. What does she want now?

I'm at the café in Richmond. I'll be here for a while, please come. Need to talk to you.

Stephanie huffed. She was slightly annoyed but did not want to let Eve down - she was developing quite a soft spot for her. She also knew that life was not always fair ... plus, Richmond was not far away.

Chapter Twenty-Six

Eve was waiting in the shop, her glasses resting on her nose.

Tam was sitting at the table too. *How strange,* thought Stephanie as she walked over to join them.

'Hi Steph, look who's here.'

'Hi Tam.'

'Hey Steph, are you going to the dance night?' Tam mumbled.

'Yeah, I am. Are you?'

'Speak up! Tam. Sometimes you're hard to understand,' Eve butted in.

'Sorry … my English is not the best. Sometimes I have to stop and think of the word in English before I speak … Anyway, I wouldn't miss the dance night for the world. I love dancing … especially with Anton.'

Eve frowned.

'Have you got a dress to wear, Stephanie?' Tam asked.

'I'm not sure what I'm going to wear. Eve has a dress.'

'Oh really?' Tam turned her attention to Eve.

'I'm wearing a red dress and thinking I'll paint my nails red too. I can't really afford to get my hair and make-up done,' Eve groaned. 'So I'll just have to do it myself … I need to cover my freckles with foundation.'

Tam started to giggle.

'What are you laughing about?'

'I don't have freckles,' Tam said. 'That's not a problem for me.'

Eve bit her lip as she picked up the menu. 'I think I'll order a hot chocolate …'

'I'm going to get a skinny latte,' Stephanie said as she handed the menu to Tam. 'What are you getting, Tam?'

'I'm sticking to the water.'

'Why don't you get green tea?' Eve suggested.

'I'll be fine with water.'

'Really …*water?*'

A young guy appeared at the end of their table.

'What can I get you ladies?'

'A hot chocolate for me,' Eve handed him the menu.

'A skinny latte, please.'

'And you?'

'I just want water.' Tam smiled at the waiter as she handed back the menu.

'She just wants water … ' Eve whispered under her breath. 'We can all see that she's watching her weight.'

The door flung open and Zara's high heels clicked as she walked along the floor. The smell of cigarette smoke wafted in her long dark hair that rested just below her bust.

'Look who just walked in,' Eve hissed.

'Let's sit here near the window,' Olivia suggested to Zara.

Tam rolled her eyes. 'I can't stand those two girls. It's so obvious that they're not at the dance school to dance.'

'What do you mean?' Eve asked.

'They want Anton's attention … They know he's single.' Tam flicked her hair over her shoulder.

'I wonder what they're doing here,' Eve snapped.

'Maybe they saw Anton?'

Eve rolled her eyes at Tam.

'I'm sure they went to visit Anton … ' Tam could not get her words out fast enough. 'Have you seen the way they look at me when I have to demonstrate dance steps with him? Zara stares me up and down.'

'Maybe they have good reasons to … ' Eve muttered under her breath.

'When she gets the chance to dance with Anton, she looks into his eyes and starts to giggle. She's such a flirt,' Tam said as she wrinkled her nose. 'They'll be at dance class tomorrow night. Makes me sick – '

'I wonder what they're going to wear to the dance night,' Eve interrupted. I'm sure Zara knows. Mmmm…You know what! I'm going to ask them.' She stood up and made her way over to the other table.

'Why is she doing that? I don't get it?' Tam whispered.

'I really don't know. Anyway, I'm going to the ladies to wash my hands,' Stephanie left the table. As she past the girls, she looked in the other direction.

The empty bathroom was the perfect place to escape. Stephanie rubbed the liquid soap gently on her hands and then placed them under the water.

'I've heard some things about you Stephanie that I'm not very happy about … '

Someone was breathing on the back of her neck. She could smell smoke. Her eyes met with an image in the mirror. It was Zara.

'Uh … what do you mean?'

'You should know.'

'Sorry Zara, I don't know what you're talking about?'

Zara gently pushed Stephanie's shoulder. Stephanie gasped but stood her ground.

'I've heard you've been spreading rumours about me,' she snapped. 'I just laugh it off … but if it ruins my chances with Anton … you're gone.' Her eyes glared at Stephanie. 'You know I mean business.'

Stephanie turned around and looked her in the eyes. 'Who told you this? I haven't said anything about you?'

'Look Stephanie, I don't leak my sources. If it's not true, that's great … but if it is, watch out. See you at dancing tomorrow night. May the best woman win.' Her nicotine breath blew into Stephanie's face as she spoke. 'I repeat, read my lips, may the best woman *win*.'

Stephanie watched Zara's bright red lips mouth the words.

Zara's skinny body wobbled out the door as she tried to balance on her high heels. Stephanie took a deep breath and followed.

'Something has come up … I have to go … sorry Eve!' Stephanie said upon returning to the table.

'But your drink has just arrived,' Eve huffed as she folded her arms. 'Stephanie, why are you going? I need to talk to you about Anton and Saturday night.'

'I'm sorry. I have to go, I'll talk to you at dancing tomorrow night.' Stephanie placed a few gold coins on the table. 'This is to pay for my coffee. See you soon, girls.'

Turning her back, she made her way out the door only to see Helena approaching her.

'Oh Stephanie, hey! I was going to see if you wanted to go for a drink after dancing but since you're here, how about now? I … I… need to talk to you about something important!'

Stephanie shrugged, 'Okay, but I can't stay too long … I'm

feeling tired and I'm not sleeping well.'

'Sorry to hear that,' Helena shook her head. 'I won't keep you long, just a quick drink. I know a bar just a few doors down from the dance school.'

A bar? Stephanie knew she was underage but figured she would just order a soft drink.

Helena's heels clunked along the footpath as the two ladies headed off.

'Here we are, let's get that table at the back. I'm having a vodka and lemonade. And you?'

'I'll just have a lemonade.'

'I'll go and get them. You take a seat.'

The smell of beer and perspiration from the men's bodies filled the room as she strolled past. Men chatted loudly at the bar, stopping every now and then to clink their glasses and drink the beer.

'Goal!' shouted a scruffy looking, middle-aged man as he stared at the television screen.

'They're a rowdy bunch,' scoffed Helena, placing the two glasses on the table. 'Now, Stephanie, I felt this couldn't wait any longer. I have noticed you've taken a liking to Anton.'

'How have you noticed that?' Stephanie could not get the words out fast enough.

'Don't worry, he's such a handsome man and all the girls like him. Everyone craves his attention and to have a crush on him is fine… I've even noticed Eve has one too… But whatever you do, don't let it be more than a crush.'

Stephanie frowned. 'Why are you telling me this? Does he have a girlfriend?'

'No, he doesn't. He likes lots of ladies. He has had so many girlfriends … I've known Anton a long time … Stephanie, I can see you're a lovely girl and I don't want you to get hurt.'

'How did you meet Anton?'

Helena's eyes looked around the bar. 'It's a long story,' she whispered.

'I want to hear about it.' Stephanie placed her arms on the table and leaned in closer.

'It began with a passion for dance. I'm not sure if I should tell you … ' Helena reached over and touched Stephanie's arm. 'I've been through so much.'

'Believe me, so have I.'

'Really?'

Stephanie nodded. 'Yes, I lost someone close to me.'

'Sorry to hear that, it's hard to lose a loved one, you never forget them. My younger sister died from childbirth. My father and I were devastated at the time. It was so hard. This tiny baby girl had been born into the world, now without a mother.'

'That would be terrible. Was the father around?'

'Gracie, she's my sister's daughter and yes, her father is still around.'

Stephanie's jaw dropped. 'So you look after Gracie?'

'Yes, Gracie is such a gorgeous girl, so determined to please everyone. She looks so much like her mother when she was growing up.'

'But where's her father?' Stephanie asked.

Helena took a deep breath and began to whisper again. 'That's my connection with Anton.'

'Anton!' Stephanie leaned back in her chair. 'Is he the father?'

'No, Bruno is.'

'Oh … so you guys are family.'

'Yes, I'm not sure if I'm proud of that or not. He pays money to me for the care of Gracie. We all moved to Australia, Bruno needed to for his work. I knew it was a better life for Gracie, as living in Spain wouldn't give her many opportunities. It all happened very suddenly.'

'But how did you meet Anton and Bruno?'

Helena sighed. 'My father was a world famous Flamenco dancer, bless his soul. He ignited a passion for dance in both my sister's and my hearts. My mother died when we were young. He was left to raise us. Over the years, my sister Camilla and I watched him perform on stage to the guitar, cello and violin. He showed so much passion in his performance. Dancing seemed to be the only thing that made him happy after my mother's death.'

'That's so sad, Helena - to have lost your mother and your sister ... but I still don't get how Anton and Bruno came into your life?'

Helena closed her eyes.

'Are you okay?' Stephanie asked.

'Yes, I'm fine, just painful memories sometimes. I have visions of Camilla and wish she was still here. Seeing Gracie everyday is a constant reminder of her.'

'Helena, I'm so sorry ... '

'Oh no, I want to tell you the rest of the story now. I remember it clearly.' Helena paused and looked at a painting on the wall of two ladies chatting at a table. 'Camilla and I were sitting at a table just like those two women in the painting. It was while my dad was rehearsing in his dance studio in Barcelona. Two young men came into the dance studio and begged my father to teach them how to dance ...

'Hello Sir, my name is Bruno and this is my younger brother Anton. We've heard that you're a world famous Flamenco dancer and we want you to teach us to dance.'

'Why should I?'

'We've travelled a long way to learn from you. We're prepared to work hard. In South America, my brother Anton was a fantastic Latin dancer. He has been dancing since he was a little boy.'

'What do you dance, Anton?'

'I dance Cha, Cha, Salsa, Rumba, Samba, Jive and Paso Doble. I have performed and taught.'

'So why have you come to me?'

'We wanted to leave South America and start a new life. Our mother was Spanish born and we want to learn Flamenco dancing.'

'I hate people wasting my time. You have a few minutes to show me what you can do…'

The two men moved their bodies to the beat. Swaying their hips from side to side, Camilla couldn't take her eyes of them.

'That's enough, I'll give you a chance.' He pointed at Anton.

'Us brothers work together, both or nothing.'

Camilla stood up from her chair and ran over to father. 'Please give them both a chance. How can you separate brothers?'

'Okay Camilla, just for you.'

'And from that day on, there was no looking back. Bruno and Camilla fell in love.'

Stephanie gently nodded to acknowledge that she had been listening.

'I didn't tell you this for sympathy,' Helena added. 'I have to get back to Gracie.'

'Okay Helena…thanks for letting me know this.'

The two ladies grabbed their bags and left.

'See you soon,' Helena said gently before she began walking in the other direction.

Stephanie sighed, she had heard so much. *Poor Helena ...*

Stephanie could relate to death and losing someone. Sitting on a nearby bench she yawned and rubbed her eyes. The train station was quite a walk. She wondered if she should call someone. Lance was the first name that entered her mind.

'Lance, it's Stephanie.'

'Hey, you need a lift?'

'Yeah, are you free?'

'No customers at the moment, where are you?'

'Richmond, close to The Vine hotel.'

'I know the one, be there in five.'

'Thanks.'

A few blokes left the pub. She shivered not wanting to give them eye contact.

Another tram past by as she continued to wait. Loneliness was quickly becoming her best friend. *I wonder what Nicole is up to,* Stephanie thought. *I should call, it's been so long.* She searched for her mobile in her bag. As she glanced at the screen, about to scroll through her contact list, the taxi arrived. She climbed in.

'What were you doing outside the pub?' Lance asked.

'I was with a friend.'

'Where is she?'

'She had to dash off.' Stephanie stared out the window.

'To Elwood?'

'Actually, I need to quickly visit a shop. Can you drive me there and then to Elwood?'

'Sure.'

'It's not far from here. A couple of blocks down.'

Lance nodded and started driving.

Stephanie gazed out the window. *What was Zara on about? Me, spreading rumours?* Stephanie thought to herself. She remembered the words that spat out of Zara's mouth like poison. *'You know I mean business...'*

'Do I need to stop soon?' Lance asked.

'Sorry! Stop here. I should not be long.'

Stephanie's hand pushed aside the dangling door decorations that covered the entrance of the crystal shop. Breathing in the sweet musky smell of burning incense she headed for the counter.

'Can I help you?'

'Is Ana here?'

'I'm so sorry. Yesterday was her last day.'

'Oh.'

'Can I help?'

'Just wanted to ask her about the rose quartz ... '

'I can help you with that,' the girl interrupted. 'Follow me.'

Stephanie glanced at the cabinets as she strolled past.

'So is Ana working somewhere else?'

'I'm not sure really. She left suddenly. One day she was here and now she's gone. Anyway, I can help you. The rose quartz is a popular crystal.'

'I'm getting it for my friend Emma.'

'Okay good choice.'

Stephanie stared at the basket full of rose quartz. The crystal was a soft pink. Emma had been so supportive recently and she wanted to give her a gift. This crystal may bring her some good luck. Stephanie reached for a medium sized crystal.

'Does that one feel right?' the girl asked.

Stephanie nodded.

'Would you like it wrapped?'

'Yes please.'

'No worries. I'll quickly put it in the bowl to clear the energy.'

Stephanie decided to look at the books while she waited –
Angel Wishes, Chakras, Happiness and Change your life.

I wish I had more time to explore, she thought.

Looking over at the window, she noticed the dream catchers.
She didn't know much about them.

'Stephanie, do you have a crystal ball reading with me?'

'Not today, Madam Farrell. I can't stay long. Just buying a gift
for my friend.'

'How lovely. Is someone helping you?'

'I was going to ask Ana but she's gone…'

'Yes Ana is no longer here… she needed to leave… but Maya
is always here to help. Anyway, better get ready for my next
reading.'

'Madam Farrell, before you leave, I was just wondering …
why do people burn incense?'

'Incense is a wonderful way to change atmosphere in a room.
It can help with meditation practice or be used in rituals.
There really are many purposes. Incense can even take a poorly
scented room and make it pleasant again. Why do you ask?'

'I overheard a man ordering an incense burner the last time
I was here.'

Madam Farrell glanced at her watch, 'Sorry Stephanie, I have
to dash off now. Need time to prepare.'

Stephanie nodded and headed back to the counter. The gift
had been wrapped. Stephanie paid, thanked the girl for her
assistance and left the shop. She did not want to keep Lance
waiting any longer.

'To Elwood now?'

Stephanie nodded.

'Did you get what you needed?'

'Yes thanks.'

'Are you ready for the dance night?'

'Kind of… the other girls are. Eve got her dress and I bet Zara knows what she's wearing.'

'Do you?'

'I have a few ideas in mind. Just want to go home now. I've had enough worrying about that.'

'Fair enough, a good sleep always helps.'

Chapter Twenty-Seven

Back at the computer again and entering more books into the catalogue, Stephanie could not get Zara's words out of her head or the image of Zara's bright red lips.

'May the best woman win ...'

'Are you okay?' Emma placed her hand on Stephanie's shoulder. 'You look deep in thought. How was the doctor's appointment?'

'Yeah, that was fine. I was just thinking about what happened after that ... '

'What happened?'

'I met a few girls from dancing for a coffee.'

'Err don't get it...did they make you a bad coffee?' Emma asked.

'No, it was the conversation we had. Everything seems so awkward around the dance people.'

'In what way?'

'I just feel like I'm in Year 9 again ... talking about this girl and that guy.'

'Guy?' Emma interrupted. 'Which guy?'

'They all talk about Anton! The dance teacher.'

'What makes everyone like him?' Emma wrinkled her nose.

'Well ... he's good-looking ... he's tall ... he can dance ...'

'Hey girls, the library is closing soon.' Ally walked over to the desk. 'I hate to break up this little party but there's still a lot to do.'

'No worries,' Emma rolled her eyes as Ally walked into the distance. 'Steph, I'll drive you home tonight. I have some news to share.'

'Okay, thank you. But wait a minute, I've got something to give you.'

Stephanie reached into her bag. The purple parcel had a silver heart stuck on the front.

'This is for you. You've been so kind to me recently.'

'Awww, you didn't have to do that. But thank you!' Emma beamed as she ripped open the paper.

'It's rose quartz, the crystal of love.'

'You're the best. Thank you so much, Steph.'

'My pleasure.'

Stephanie rubbed her arms as she sat in Emma's car seat.

'I'll put the heating on, yeah?'

'Yeah, thanks. I'm freezing.'

'Okay, so, I have some good and bad news. The good news, Oliver and I have arranged the date ... but the bad news, it's for Friday. I know it's tomorrow but he's busy with band practice and it's been hard to lock in a time. Are you free?'

'I have dancing on Friday night.'

'Come on, Steph! Just miss one class. Please do this for me.'

'Okay ... but I still haven't checked with Daniel.'

'Oh ... I thought you had ...'

'I haven't checked the app in a couple of days.' Stephanie

reached for her phone and checked her messages. 'Oh, whoops, he replied.'

'And …'

'He likes the idea … but tomorrow is such late notice, don't you think?'

'Just explain the situation.'

'Mmm … okay. I'll message him now.' Stephanie typed a message and hit send.

The Toyota Corolla pulled into the curb.

'Guess we'll just have to wait for an answer. Let me know ASAP.'

'Hang on, he just replied.'

'What did he say, what did he say?'

'"Sounds good, send the details through."'

'Pass it here,' Emma said while grabbing the phone out of Stephanie's hands.

'Done! Details sent. Thanks Steph, this means so much to me. I can't wait for you to meet Oliver!'

'It should be fun,' Stephanie said with half a smile. *What have I gotten myself into?* she thought.

Stephanie wanted to look sexy.

A black skirt and a lacy top lay on her dressing table. She had pulled them out of her wardrobe before she had left for work. She wanted to be ready for her dance class.

Reaching for the bottle of Chanel, she sprayed the sweet fragrance onto her neck. *I hope Anton notices me…*

Applying black eyeliner on the top of her eyelids and a berry lipstick, her features were defined. Her hair hung past her shoulders and this was the way she would leave it. Spraying her fringe to give it more style, her look was complete. She now felt sexy. Stephanie could hear the sound of raindrops hitting against her window. She didn't want to walk to the station in the rain. *Lance it is,* she decided as she reached for her phone and hit call.

'Stephanie, how are you?'

'I'm fine, can you drive me to dance class?'

'Where are you calling from?'

'I'm at home. Can you pick me up at the Elwood shopping strip?'

'Sure, see you in ten minutes.'

She hurried along the street to the shopping strip to meet Lance. To her surprise, he was already there waiting for her.

'That was quick,' Stephanie said.

'Yeah, I was in the area.'

Stephanie nodded but did not respond.

Lance drove slowly as he did not want the tyres to slip on the wet road. Water was splashing up everywhere as the cars drove madly around him.

'So, what made you decide to go to these classes?' Lance asked.

'I've always loved dancing but had never tried Latin dancing. It's quite different to anything I've ever done.'

'How so?'

'In Latin dancing, you dance with a partner. I never did that in jazz, tap or ballet.'

'Are there a lot of guys in the class?'

'A few guys but definitely more girls – '

'Young guys?' Lance butted in.

'Not really, Anton is probably the youngest guy. I think he's in his mid to late twenties. Not sure really.'

'So all the guys are older?'

'Yeah, they are,' replied Stephanie. What's with all the strange questions?

'Oh, guess what! I got the tickets for Dirty Dancing.'

'Nice. Who are you going with?'

'My mum… remember how I told you she was an actress and likes the theatre. Well, it's part of her birthday present. I'm flying her over to Melbourne for the weekend.'

'That's really sweet, Lance. Great present.'

'Yeah, I think so. Here we are.'

Stephanie stared out the window at the dance school. Zara was standing out the front.

'Now, will you need a lift home?'

'I think so.'

'Just call me when you're finished. Enjoy the dance class.'

'Thanks.'

Zara glared at the taxi as she leaned against the street pole. Puffing on her cigarette, she watched Stephanie head for the door.

'You're coming Saturday night, Stephanie?' Becky asked as she handed the change over.

'Yep, I'm coming.'

'Hi Becky,' Zara pushed Stephanie aside. 'Sorry, I didn't see you there, Stephanie.'

Olivia started to giggle.

'You need to grow taller or wear some heels. Becky, do you like the colour I painted my nails? It's called Satan's Kiss.'

Stephanie turned her back and made her way over to the couch. Looking across the dance floor, she could see Anton talking to Helena. They were deep in conversation. Within minutes, Zara and Olivia had joined the wolf pack. Zara's arm was making its way over Anton's shoulder, as she hunted for his attention. Stephanie turned her head to find Harvey sitting next to her.

'Hey Stephanie, are you coming on Saturday night?' Harvey asked.

'Yeah, I am.'

'Are you coming alone?'

'No, a group of us are coming.'

'Is Eve coming with you?' Harvey started to move his body closer to hers. His hand reached out to touch her.

'I'm here, Stephanie! I need to tell you something.' Eve grabbed Stephanie's hand. 'Come with me.'

Stephanie followed Eve into the bathroom.

'Jeez that Harvey is a creep! Good thing I arrived. Anyway, I'm ready for Saturday night, I have it all planned. Anton is sure to notice me. I'm not telling anyone what I'm going to do because I don't trust the other girls … but I need your help with – '

'Hi ladies…'

It was Helena.

'Oh, hi Helena,' said Stephanie.

'Are you ready for Saturday night?' Helena asked.

'I am!' Eve snapped.

'And you, Stephanie?'

'Yes, I think I know what I'm going to wear.'

Eve began to make her way out the door. 'See you in class, Steph.'

'Is she okay?' Helena frowned.

Stephanie shrugged. 'She's fine.'

'That's good. Let's get on the dance floor. Class should be starting soon.'

Tam, Eve, Zara and Olivia had already positioned themselves closely behind Anton.

'You're a bit close ... ' Anton threw up his hand. 'Just stand back a bit so you can watch the steps. I think we'll try the Rumba tonight. This is known for being a slow dance. Some people may think of it as the dance of love,' Anton hesitated. 'People may pretend they're in love.' He smiled widely. 'The movements are a lot slower than the Salsa. Anyway, let's give it a go. Watch my movements.'

Swaying his hips, Anton stepped to the side. The beams of light lit up his smiling face and cheeky eyes.

'Slow movements ... That's right, Zara, you've got it ... Moving well there, Tam ... Okay, let's pair up. Girls move to the left side and boys on the right.'

The girls rushed over to the left side trying to be the closest female to Anton, hoping to be his first dance. Zara huffed, rolled her eyes and flicked her hair, as she did not get to stand opposite Anton. Eve giggled as she was there first.

Anton stared at Eve, 'Actually ... I'll choose who will pair up. Tam, you can demonstrate with me since you've been learning the Rumba for a while. Helena with Con, Harvey with Olivia, Jacob with Eve, sorry, forgot your name but you can stand in that gap ... Steph, you stand in the space next to me and just follow along when the music starts.'

Gently, Anton began to move the lower half of his body. Tam followed his lead. 'Change partners,' Anton dropped his hand and held it out to Stephanie. A tiny smirk appeared on his face. 'Do you feel sexy?' Anton whispered into her ear. 'You're blushing.'

Stephanie looked into his eyes and then away from him. Anton's feet stopped and he dropped her hands.

'Move on. My next victim is Eve.'

Eve stood in front of Anton. She held her hands up ready to dance. Stephanie looked back at Anton as she slowly walked over to Jacob who had a big smile on his face.

'That was a quick dance, Anton,' Zara blurted out.

'You'll be dancing with me next, Zara.'

'You look red in the face Stephanie. You okay?' Jacob asked as they held a tight grip.

'I'm not used to the Rumba movements yet.'

'You'll be fine. Just let me lead and you follow along.'

Jacob's bulky frame held Stephanie's lanky body firmly. The movements felt quite tight and forceful. He had the power and control. Stephanie's arms ached as she tried to relax.

'I think you may feel more comfortable if you sway and relax your hips more.'

'It's different dancing with you, Jacob. You're a lot shorter than Anton.'

'Ha, we all know Anton is a giant but age and wisdom over youth any day' his eyes focused on hers.

'Zara, you're with me now, Stephanie and Jacob you need to change partners.' Anton said.

Stephanie stared at Anton and Zara as they danced the steps. His twinkling eyes were focused on Zara as she played with her long curly locks. Mouthing some words, she then licked her lips and rested her hands in his. Leaning in closer, she tried to move her hips against his.

Stephanie looked away and continued to allow her own feet to move to the beat of the music. Stepping to the right, she tried to slowly move her hips and imagine she was dancing with a partner. *I can do this.* She began to smile as she focused on herself. The stiffness in her shoulders lessened as her body started to relax. She then allowed her hips to move more freely.

Now she was in the spotlight and her dark hair shone under the lights.

Anton stopped directly in front of her. 'We'll have to leave it there for tonight, folks. I hope you've enjoyed the Rumba. Don't forget Saturday night, time to dance and party.'

'I can't wait,' Zara said as she stood next to Anton, flicking her hair to one side.

'Excuse me, Anton,' Stephanie tapped him on the shoulder. 'I won't be at class tomorrow night.'

'Why not, Steph?'

'I've something else on … but I'll be coming on Saturday.'

'Okay, don't forget to bring your dance shoes.'

Eve grabbed Stephanie's arm. 'Did Anton just wink at you?'

'I'm not sure.'

'I'm sure he did and did you see Zara dancing the Rumba with him? She was all over him and she couldn't stop giggling. *Damn her!* Tam was trying her best to get him to notice her too.'

'Eve! Come here,' Zara waved her over.

Stephanie watched the group of girls from a distance. The group burst into laughter. Eve had a huge smile on her face.

'Do you want to practice dancing?' a hand rested on Stephanie's shoulder. 'I think we should.'

Turning around to face the figure, her eyes met Jacob. 'I'm just waiting for Eve. She shouldn't be long.'

'Looks like she's leaving now with the other girls.'

'I have to go.' Stephanie made her exit and reached the bottom step without looking back.

The dark sky reflected her mood. She could see the group of girls ahead of her. *Lance, I must call Lance,* Stephanie thought.

'Hi, can you please pick me up now? I've finished my dance class.'

It was as if Lance had been waiting for her call.

'Sure. I'm quite close by, actually. I'll be there soon.'

'Thank you.'

Stephanie sighed, she hoped she would not have to wait long at least it had stopped raining.

'Stephanie … '

She could hear footsteps right behind her.

'Stephanie, stop!'

She spun around.

'Jacob! You gave me a fright. I thought you were still upstairs.'

'Nah, I've had enough dancing. Can I drive you somewhere?' he asked.

'Someone's coming to pick me up.'

'Should I wait with you?' Jacob continued to stare at Stephanie.

'I should be fine,' Stephanie hesitated.

'Who's coming to get you? Your boyfriend?' He smiled widely.

Stephanie raised her eyebrows. 'No, just a friend.'

'So, you're coming on Saturday night?' Jacob continued.

'Yes,' Stephanie did not know what else to say. 'Here's my lift.'

'A taxi?'

'Yeah, see ya.' With those last words, Stephanie dashed over to the car.

'Who was that?' Lance asked.

'Jacob from dancing,' Stephanie said as she locked her door.

'He looks old.'

'I told you there aren't many young guys.'

'What did he want?'

'He was just wondering how I was getting home.' Stephanie fastened her seat beat.

'Was he trying to offer you a lift?'

'Not sure, I told him someone was picking me up.'

'Makes you wonder what brought him to the dance class … '

'I guess … I never thought about that. Maybe he just loves to dance.'

'Did he dance with you tonight?'

'Yeah, you change partners all the time.'

'I see … '

The two sat in silence for a few minutes.

'Just drop me off here, thanks Lance.'

'Are you sure? I can drop you at your house.'

'No, just at the shops. I might go into the supermarket.'

Stephanie had no intention of going into the shop but she had enough of Lance's strange questions.

Chapter Twenty-Eight

'Stephanie, what are you going to wear tonight?' Emma asked as they left the library.

'I haven't had much of a chance to think about it, Em. I was at dancing last night.'

'Are you kidding me? That's all I've thought about! I'm so excited.'

'What are you going to wear?'

'I've tried on so many outfits but nothing seemed to look right. Then I thought, what's my favourite colour? Red. So I started to look for red outfits and then I found one.'

'And what was that?' Stephanie asked.

'My red dress with white polka dots. It looks good with my red hair,' Emma giggled.

'I think I've seen you wear that dress before.'

'You have. I wore it when we went to the movies a few weeks back. It's a little dressy but I don't care. Polka dots are so in right now.' Emma smiled widely. 'You know how to get to the restaurant, yeah?'

'Yeah, I do. I'll see you later.' Stephanie exchanged a smile with her friend.

'I'm so excited. See you in Lygon Street!' Emma shouted

across the road as she waved goodbye to Stephanie.

'Mum can I ask you a favour?' Stephanie walked into the kitchen.

'You look nice, Stephanie. Are you going somewhere?'

'Yeah, I'm going out to dinner. Can you drive me?'

'Of course, is this dinner with friends?'

'I'm going on a date … '

'A date, how exciting! But I hope you're meeting in a public place?'

Stephanie nodded. 'It's okay, Mum. Em is coming too. It's a double date.'

'Oh, lovely! She seems to have taken you under her wing. I like her, she is such a good girl. So when do you need to leave?'

'Soon, if that's okay.'

'I'll just finish up here and then take you.'

Lygon Street was always busy as many people loved to dine there. Stephanie looked in her mirror as her mother drove. She had not bothered to apply any makeup for the date.

'Can you just drop me off here, please?'

'Sure, now do I need to pick you up?'

'Nah, all good. I'm getting a lift with Emma.'

'Have a lovely time, darling!'

'Thanks Mum.'

Stephanie could see Emma standing in the distance.

Emma's red hair hung just past her shoulders and her fringe rested on the top of her eyebrows. She was staring into a small mirror.

'Just checking to see how I look for our double date. I arrived twenty minutes early. I've been chatting to Oliver for weeks now,' she giggled. 'I like that he's a drummer…I usually wouldn't go for a musician but his conversation and witty personality have really reeled me in. Do you want to have a look in the mirror?'

'No thanks. Hey, can you drop me home? I didn't want to ask Mum to come and get me.'

'Sure. Are you okay? You look nervous?'

Stephanie avoided eye contact. 'A little, I guess.'

'This is going to be fun,' Emma said as she grabbed Stephanie's arm. 'Let's go inside.'

A man tossed some dough in the air as the two girls passed the wood fired oven.

'Can you smell the garlic?'

'Don't worry, I brought some mints.'

'Do you have a reservation?' The waiter asked.

'Yes, under Emma, 7pm, for four people. We're a little bit early.'

'That's fine, follow me please.'

'What a lovely table right by the window.' Emma was impressed. 'Might message Oliver now, let him know we're at Table 11.'

'Now, can I bring you any water? Still or tap?' the waiter asked.

Emma took a seat. 'Tap, thanks. Listen to the music Steph, is that Andrea Bocelli's song playing?'

'Who's he?' Stephanie wrinkled her nose.

'An Italian singer,' Emma giggled.

Stephanie placed her serviette on her lap. 'Shows how much I know about music.'

Candlelight lit the room as the restaurant diners chatted. Emma held the menu in front of her. 'Yum, chicken risotto with mushroom. I love risotto!'

Stephanie eyed the menu. 'I'll probably go for pasta.'

'I wonder what Oliver will choose. I'm not sure if he's a big fan of Italian food, I guess that's all part of the mystery. Look at the dessert menu. They have my favourite!'

'Let me guess … ' Stephanie muttered, 'chocolate something?'

'Chocolate cake!' Emma licked her lips.

'Don't do that,' Stephanie started to giggle.

'I'm just dreaming about it now.'

A bowl with prawns and pasta passed their table, Stephanie knew that's what Andrew would have ordered.

'Is this Table 11?'

'Sure is,' Emma said, grinning ear to ear.

'Hey, I'm Oliver … '

'I'm Emma … finally, we get to meet.' Her face flushed pink as she batted her eyelashes.

'This is for you.'

Emma looked at the rectangular blue box. 'I love chocolates, thank you so much.'

'I know,' Oliver grinned.

'This is my friend, Stephanie.'

'Nice to meet ya.' Oliver shot a smile at Stephanie.

'Her date should be here soon.' Emma looked at her watch. 'It's just 7 now.'

'Mmm, smells good. I can't wait to try the food. I've never been to this place,' Oliver said as he sat down at the table.

'Here's the menu.'

'Thanks, Emma.'

Emma nudged Stephanie under the table. She could not stop

smiling. 'Oliver, I was telling Stephanie that you're a drummer and you play in a band … '

'Yeah, I've been playing the drums since I was ten. My cousin asked me to play at his sixteenth birthday and that's when the band started. There's Jack who plays guitar, I'm on drums and Richard's our singer. Jack and I went to school together and I met Richard through a friend.'

Emma sighed. 'I would love to hear your band play some day.'

'For sure, that's my night job. During the day I'm a gardener. I spend my days mowing lawns and pulling out weeds.'

'I didn't know that … I guess I've been so busy talking to you about the band,' Emma giggled. 'I can find you a good book on gardening or maybe Steph can. We both work at the library – '

'Hey guys … ' a man interrupted their conversation. 'Sorry I'm late. I'm Daniel.'

A man in a grey suit with blonde wavy hair and dreamy blue eyes stood at the end of the table.

'Stephanie?'

'That's me,' Stephanie croaked. She felt her throat go dry.

'I recognise you from your photo. Pleased to meet you.' He handed her a bunch of orchids.

'How sweet,' Emma mouthed.

Stephanie gazed at the petals and breathed in the sweet fragrance. Someone special had given her roses before and had told her that they were a symbol of love. She brushed away the pieces of hair that fell in her face.

'Thank you so much,' she said.

'My pleasure,' Daniel said with a smile.

'I should have thought of flowers,' Oliver groaned.

'I'm Emma and this is Oliver,' said Emma, interrupting the moment.

'Nice to meet you,' Daniel said as he sat in the empty seat opposite Stephanie. 'Can I get some wine for the table? What do you like Stephanie?'

'I think I'll just have a soft drink, if that's okay.'

Stephanie cringed she did not want to take the risk of underage drinking at a licensed restaurant.

'I'll get a lemonade. I'm on my P plates,' Emma butted in.

'And you, mate?'

'Yeah, I'll have a wine.'

'Just one minute, I'll go and speak to the waiter. What soft drink, Stephanie?' he asked.

'Lemonade, please.'

'He's cute,' Emma whispered. 'And I like the flowers too.'

Oliver folded his arms. 'What does he do for a crust?'

'Didn't you say he was a lawyer?'

'That's right.' Stephanie muttered.

Oliver rolled his eyes. 'Yeah, that explains the suit. Must have come straight from work. You'll hardly ever catch me in a suit.'

'Well, that's fixed.' Daniel joined them back at the table. 'Sorry I'm late but I had to organise something at work and I just couldn't leave earlier. At least Lygon Street wasn't too far.'

'Where do you work?' Emma asked.

'Just in the city.'

'That's handy. Stephanie and I work close to the beach. Do you know Hampton?'

'I do.'

'Yeah, we work in Hampton – '

'My band plays in the city all the time,' Oliver interrupted.

'You're a musician? Daniel started to butter his bread roll.

'Yeah, at night I play drums in a band and during the day I'm a gardener. I heard you're a lawyer?'

Daniel shrugged. 'Yeah, it doesn't give me much time to do anything else. I do like gardens but a lot of my time is spent in the office.'

'Have you seen many bands play?' Oliver rested his arms on the table.

'Not really, I'm not much of a music person.'

'Are you ready to order?' the waitress asked.

'Are we?' Emma reinforced.

'Yes, let's go ahead. Ladies first … '

The orders were taken and they began chatting again.

'I've never been here before.' Oliver said.

'It's not a bad place I'm actually looking forward to my dessert.' Emma looked at Daniel. 'Do you like desserts?'

'I'm not a big fan of dessert. More savoury foods, I'm a bit of a plain eater – chicken, fish and rice dishes.'

Emma hesitated. 'Mmm, Stephanie maybe I made the wrong choice by suggesting Italian?'

'Oh no, it's always nice to try something different,' Oliver interrupted.

'Here's the wine and the lemonades. Shall I pour a little bit in your glass, sir?' the waiter asked.

'Yes, please.'

Daniel swished the wine around in his glass, gave it a sniff and sipped it.

'Very nice, thank you.'

'You're not drinking wine ladies?' The waiter asked.

'Not for me,' Stephanie said.

'No thanks,' Emma mouthed.

Oliver nodded as he held out his glass.

'Cheers to a good night,' Daniel raised his glass.

'Cheers.'

'The food will not be long.'

Stephanie listened to the others chat. Emma spoke about movies she had watched and Oliver told them more about his band. Daniel nodded giving Stephanie a smile.

'Here's your food. Would anyone like some cheese?' asked the waitress.

'No, thank you.'

'Not for me.'

Oliver waved his hand. 'Yep, over here, thanks! I love my cheese.'

Emma began eyeing off his plate. 'Oliver, that looks good and I love cheese too but not on chicken risotto.'

'Is that enough cheese, sir?' the waitress asked.

'Can you just leave it on the table? Thanks.'

Stephanie watched the steam rise from the spaghetti bolognaise in front of her.

'Yours looks good, Stephanie,' Daniel commented.

'I love a good pasta dish. I also like chocolate but didn't think I could fit dessert in as well.'

'I thought I would try the fish as it came with vegetables as well. I can't eat chocolate cake. I'm a diabetic,' Daniel sighed.

'That's a big piece of fish mate! I should have ordered that,' announced Oliver with his mouth half full.

'It does look nice, I must say.'

The four diners chatted pleasantly throughout the main course and soon the dessert arrived.

Oliver eyeballed his plate. 'Look at the chocolate cake!'

'It's definitely the best one I've seen, Oliver.' Emma picked up her spoon and placed it into her mouth.

'This is amazing, so rich and moist,' she said between mouthfuls. 'Stephanie, do you want to try?'

'No thanks, Em. I'm so full, but it looks delicious.'

'I love chocolate way too much… Can never say no!'

'Me too,' Oliver said as he scooped up the last mouthful of his chocolate cake. 'Emma … let's order another one. We can share it.'

'That sounds like a good idea!'

'I'll order it with two spoons and an extra scope of ice cream.' Daniel looked at his watch. 'I'm really sorry but I'm going to have to leave soon. I have to go into the office tomorrow.'

'You have to work on Saturday morning?' Oliver frowned.

'Yes, unfortunately. There's always so much to do. I need to plan a holiday sometime and get away. That will only happen when it gets quieter but that won't be for a while.'

Oliver nodded. 'I can't remember the last time I went on a holiday. It would have to be a few years ago.'

Daniel sighed. 'Please excuse me, I'll get this.'

Emma gasped. 'You don't have to do – '

'All good, Emma.'

'Thank you,' Stephanie muttered.

'No, it's my pleasure.' Daniel stood up and made his way to the counter.

'He didn't even give me a chance to offer,' Oliver huffed.

'Don't worry Oliver. It's a good excuse for another outing,' Emma reassured. 'Oh how sweet, Steph! He must like you.'

'Stop Emma! He's coming back.'

Daniel smiled at Stephanie when he returned to the table.

'Thanks for a great night, guys.'

'Yeah, I think we all had a good time,' Emma said, smiling widely. 'We should do it again.'

'I would like to. Stephanie, I'll contact you soon.'

'Yeah, sure.'

He gently touched Stephanie on the shoulder.

'Look forward to hearing from you,' Stephanie grinned.

What did I just say? she wondered. *Is this really what I want? Or am I just being polite?*

Daniel grinned. 'Bye for now. Enjoy your evening everyone.'

Stephanie rested back into the chair.

The rest of the night was spent listening to Emma and Oliver making trivial conversation. Stephanie was glad when Emma finally decided to call it a night.

Chapter Twenty-Nine

Saturday night had finally arrived.

Stephanie had been looking forward to this for so long — another chance to dance with Anton.

Last night Daniel had been the perfect gentleman. But Anton was always on her mind. There was something about Anton… something mysterious…

Stephanie took the blue dress from her wardrobe. The lacy flower print had attracted her to buy it in the first place. The other dress she chose was a plain black one with a little sparkle through the material. Her black heels matched this outfit better so it seemed like the more sensible choice.

The black dress hugged her figure. Stephanie yawned as she stared into the mirror. Her pale skin juxtaposed her rose tinted lips that longed to be kissed again. Picking up her comb, she brushed the tangled pieces of her dark hair. *So much to do and not enough time…*

Stephanie made her way into the bathroom. Her hot pink make-up bag rested on the marble bench. Pulling the zipper on the bag, she reached for a bottle and tipped the brown liquid onto the palm of her hand. *Ohhh…haven't done that for a while…*

She applied the foundation to her face with a soft sponge, rubbing it gently against her cheeks. This made her pale complexion turn into a bronzy one. *Much better…*

Next she held the long skinny pencil between her fingers. She applied the black to the bottom of her eyelids. Her blue eyes were a contrast to the black curly lashes. Her rose tinted lips needed to come to life. Moving her mouth, she gently applied the raspberry coloured gloss onto her upper lip and then the lower one. Now she was ready. Ready to face Anton. *I hope he notices me….*

The taxi she had called, pulled up directly in front of the venue.

'Rendezvous Restaurant is right there. Twenty dollars.'

'Thanks.' Stephanie handed over the money

'Have a good night.'

Stephanie closed the car door. *I wonder if anyone is here yet?*

Not wanting to be first she stood on the street and stared up into the night sky. Looking at the moon reminded her of *The Undiscovered Worlds of Peru* – the Incas and sacrifice being part of their culture.

'We're here …' Zara announced as she walked past with Olivia pulling down her tight skirt.

'I hope you get to dance with Anton!'

'I will … '

Stephanie waited a moment and then went inside.

Damn … Just my luck. Zara will get there first …

Stephanie climbed the red-carpeted staircase, tightly holding the railing, as she did not want to trip. Becky was standing at the top step.

'Hey Stephanie, I'm directing our guests to their tables.' A black folder rested on a table beside her. 'You're on Table 19. Have a great night.'

Stephanie sighed and made her way into the unfamiliar room. Many round tables covered with white cloths occupied the brightly lit reception room. Red, orange, yellow and black balloons formed the centre piece on each table. As Stephanie searched for her table, her image was reflected in the many mirrors that hung on the cream walls.

'Is this Table 19?' she said to a middle-aged lady.

'Yes, it is.'

A few empty chairs surrounded the table. Stephanie pulled out the grey backed seat and sat comfortably on the red cushion. *Where is he?* she thought.

There he was, standing on the polished floorboards surrounded by women. Smiling and chatting, the women were all competing for his attention. Anton stroked his black velvet jacket while the girls held out their iPhones trying to take photos.

'Anton, have a photo with me!'

One girl posed while the other one took the photo.

I wonder if he'll speak to me, Stephanie thought.

A sweet fragrance drifted in the air as some more girls in slinky dresses and heels wobbled past the table.

'Watch where you're going!'

One of the girls had bumped straight into another. Her eyes had been focused on Anton and not on where she was going. It was Eve.

'Sorry.'

Eve was with another girl with long blonde hair and pale skin. This girl was wearing a purple dress that barely covered her behind. Stephanie wondered if this was Louise, who Eve had spoken about. Eve clearly had not noticed Stephanie and was pulling the blonde girl's arm and heading in the direction of Anton. Stephanie thought she would speak to Eve later.

Anton continued to prance around the room like a peacock, holding his head high. His black and white striped shirt complemented his crushed velvet jacket, tight fitting black pants and polished black shoes.

Stephanie watched the scene in front of her. There were so many girls trying to get Anton's attention. She glanced at the table next to her, noticing a girl who had her hands on her hips and was batting her eyelashes. A smile was plastered across her drawn face as she eyed all the men that passed her.

Zara ...

'Anton,' she grabbed his arm as he walked past. 'Do you want a vodka shot?'

'Not now, Zara. I have to dance but I'll have a drink later.'

Zara pulled his body closer to her as she tried to gaze into his eyes. Her long locks hung below her skinny chin.

Looking at her sharp features, he smiled. 'I'll be back later.'

'I'll have a vodka shot while I'm waiting for you, perhaps I'll even get to see that bird tattoo if I'm lucky,' she cooed.

Anton passed Stephanie's table but failed to acknowledge her.

Stephanie could see Tam sitting over at Table 8. The down light caught the sparkle of her red beaded dress. Stephanie waved to Tam and the gesture was returned.

The black speakers started to vibrate as the music began. The pulsating Latin beat filled the room. Under the table, Stephanie began to move her feet, marking out the Salsa steps.

'Ladies and gentlemen, welcome to Dance Discovery's social night! My name is Bruno Lorenzo and I'll be your MC for the night,' a loud voice bellowed into the microphone. 'Tonight, we're here to dance. And, of course, to see the fabulous Anton perform.'

'Anton!' screamed a girl sitting at a table in front of the stage.

'Yes, you said it girl! Anton will be performing and if you're lucky you may even get to dance with him later.'

Stephanie sighed. *I want to dance with Anton …*

'After that, there will be a chance for everyone to get up on the dance floor and do some Latin dancing Salsa, Jive, Rumba and Cha, Cha. So sit back and enjoy your night!'

The audience broke into applause.

Zara pushed her chair against Stephanie's. 'I want the best view of Anton,' she said to Olivia. 'Pour me another vodka shot … Cheers!

Stephanie heard their glasses clink then watched as they placed the empty glasses on the table.

'Take one of these,' Zara said as she handed something to Olivia.

'Where did you get that, Zara?'

'Anton gave it to me,' she said as she handed the white tablet to Olivia. He sells them all the time. You should get into it too. You get a better deal if you are a regular client.'

Stephanie tried not to turn her head too much but leaned in a little closer to hear the conversation. She wondered why Zara had been at the dance studio the other night. She was sure that she hadn't had a private lesson. *Mind your own business Stephanie,* she thought.

'Whatever Anton says …' Olivia placed the tablet on her tongue, picked up her glass and swallowed the drug.

'Anton's so sexy,' Zara purred as she flicked her hair over her shoulder. 'Have you seen his tattoo?'

'No?'

'I love guys with tattoos – it's of a bird. I'll ask him to show us later, it's a good excuse for him to take off his shirt – he loves to do that. I hope my lipstick still looks decent.' Zara grabbed her handbag and started to check for a mirror.

'Are you going to eat your bread roll, Zara?' Olivia asked, changing the subject.

'Are you kidding me? I have to watch my weight. Anton's not into big girls,' Zara scoffed as she handed the bread roll to Olivia. 'You have it.'

The lights suddenly dimmed.

'Please welcome Anton and Isabella to the dance floor,' Bruno announced.

Anton made his way to the centre of the polished wooden dance floor, holding hands with a tall female wearing a black dress with orange frills along the hemline. Her brown hair was tied back neatly in a bun. Anton elevated his body and held his chin up ready to begin the dance routine.

The two dancers moved smoothly around the dance floor swaying their hips from side to side and mirroring each other's bodies. Step, spin and sway. The dance movements were very suggestive. Gazing into each other's eyes, Anton pulled his partner closer to his body.

Stephanie gasped.

Isabella placed her hands on her hips and shook her head from side to side. Anton touched the side of her body and then spun her around. Together they glided further across the floor.

Isabella looks so sexy, she thought. *They have a strong connection when they dance. I wish that was me …*

Anton's unbuttoned his shirt, revealing his toned and tanned body. Bright white lights flashed from cameras. Anton spun Isabella out for the final dance movement. She curtseyed and he bowed to the applauding audience. Leaving the floor, Anton and Isabella smiled and waved to the appreciative crowd.

'There you have it! Aren't they brilliant dancers, Anton and

Isabella,' Bruno kept clapping. 'Soon it will be your turn. Sit back, relax and enjoy the night.' Bruno put the microphone down and left the stage.

The music started again. Stephanie listened to the strong rhythmic beat and her toes began tapping again on the floor.

'Watch out.'

Zara at the next table had moved her chair hard against Stephanie's to make her way onto the dance floor. The tightly fitted electric pink dress hugged her bony figure. Wobbling all over the place, she joined the crowd of dancers who had taken over the dance floor.

Stephanie watched Eve, Louise and Helena on the floor. Harvey was nearby. His eyes were fixed on Eve.

Should I go over … No mind your own business … she thought.

Anton appeared on the floor and the three females started to make their moves, gravitating towards him. A grin appeared on his face as he eyed them up and down. He danced with many girls.

Stephanie wiped her forehead and decided to leave the table.

'Excuse me, where are the ladies toilets?' she asked the waitress.

'Just over there.'

'Thank you.'

Chapter Thirty

Stephanie stared into the mirror, carefully reapplying her lipstick.

'Steph, sorry I haven't had a chance to speak to you.'

'Oh Eve, there you are. I saw you dancing on the dance floor but thought I would talk to you later.'

'I'm having so much fun. I've already spoken to Anton. Look, he gave me this.' Eve opened her hand, a tiny white tablet lay on her palm. 'I'm just about to take it. Down it goes! He said it will help me and I should get more.'

Help you ... with what? Stephanie wondered as Eve reapplied some red lipstick and then brushed her long hair.

'Anyway, no time to chat, I need to get back to Anton. I want a photo with him. And if this helps me, I may get some more. Have a good night, Steph. I might speak to you later.'

'But Eve – '

The door slammed shut.

While walking back to her table, Stephanie spotted Eve on the dance floor with Anton. *Perhaps Eve had a headache and asked Anton for a tablet? But Anton gave some to Zara too ... that was no Panadol.* She felt a hand on her shoulder.

'Are you enjoying your night?'

Lance's blue eyes stared into hers. He had never looked at her in this way before. Stephanie looked down at his hand as it rested on her shoulder. She let out a small gasp – half of his little finger was missing.

Noticing the shock on her face, Lance quickly removed his hand from Stephanie's shoulder.

'Um … yeah, it's been okay,' she mumbled, feeling quite startled.

Lance sat in the empty seat beside her.

'Are you going to get up and dance?'

Stephanie shook her head. 'Maybe in a little while, you surprised me Lance, I didn't know you were here.'

'I arrived not that long ago.' Sitting back in his chair he smiled briefly at her before changing the subject. 'So … I'm guessing that's Anton in the middle of the dance floor?'

'Yeah … that's him.'

'And the guy holding the microphone?'

'That's Bruno, Anton's brother.'

There was an awkward silence.

Why is he asking me this? she wondered.

'So does Bruno dance too?'

'Not sure really, Anton's the dance teacher – '

'But they run the business together?' Lance interrupted.

'Yes I think so.'

'I wonder what he does …' Lance whispered under his breath.

Stephanie ignored the comment and continued to stare at the girls on the dance floor.

'Look at those girls!' Lance said. 'They're so drunk, wobbling all over the place. Party girls …' he hesitated, 'only good for one thing. Ha! Look at them now, trying to pull their dresses down so they don't reveal anything.' He burst into laughter.

Stephanie didn't find his comment funny at all.

'Lance, they were drinking heaps of vodka at the table before and ... They were ... '

'They were what?' Lance stared at Stephanie.

Stephanie leaned closer to him. 'I think they were taking drugs,' she whispered.

'Drugs!'

'Shhh! Keep your voice down,' Stephanie muttered. 'I heard them say they got it from Anton ... but I don't want to believe that.'

Folding his arms, Lance looked back onto the dance floor. 'Come with me,' he said as he gently took Stephanie's hand.

Lance guided Stephanie through the reception centre and down the red-carpeted staircase. Stephanie gasped as she grabbed the railing.

'What happened?' Lance asked.

'I nearly lost my balance.'

'You okay?'

'Yeah, I'm just not used to wearing high heels.'

They made their way through the front door and onto the street. The cold air rested on Stephanie's shoulders as she stared into the night sky.

'We needed to come outside so no one can hear us,' Lance murmured.

Water splashed onto Stephanie's leg as a car raced by.

'Did you see that?' boomed Lance, raising his hand at the car. 'The car just went through the red light, crazy driver! He could have killed us!'

'Yeah, I saw,' she said as she leaned on the ticket machine for support. 'Where did you park?'

'Around the corner in the car park, couldn't get a spot out

the front. I don't think you have to pay at this time of the night.'

'That's good.'

'And you?'

'I got dropped off.'

'So you may need a lift home?'

'Maybe … depends.'

Lance frowned but did not continue to follow through with the conversation.

Stephanie just wanted to go back inside. Pain shot down her legs. Again, she noticed his little finger.

'What happened?'

Lance frowned. 'Huh?'

'Your finger.'

Lance held out his hand for Stephanie to have a closer look. 'Had an accident.'

Stephanie took a quick glance and then looked away.

'One night I was using a butcher's knife to cut some steak. I lost concentration for a second and, bang, this happened in one slice.'

Stephanie went weak in the knees. She wanted to vomit at that thought.

'I don't like seeing blood.'

'It was bleeding a hell of a lot!'

'Stop! No more, please.'

Lance laughed. 'Okay, so, change of topic …' he turned his head to check there was no one around. 'I thought there was something funny about Anton but I was not sure what it was. I think we have to tell someone about this.'

'No!' Stephanie gasped. 'We can't. It's none of our business.'

'But Stephanie, it's wrong. Drugs are illegal and he's stuffing up people's lives.'

'We don't know the whole story,' she snapped. 'We have no proof that Anton gave them drugs. They may even be lying.'

'Stephanie, I think we should investigate further. Maybe I'll go and have a chat to the girls.'

'No, please don't do that. They're all in love with him.' She grabbed his arm.

'So what? That's not a good reason not to talk to them about it. If it's not Anton, maybe it's Bruno ... or maybe the two brothers are working together.'

Stephanie sighed she did not know what to do.

'Look, maybe we should go back upstairs and talk to them together.' Lance suggested.

'Are you okay out here?' called a voice.

Bruno stood at the door.

'Yeah ... all good, Bruno.' Stephanie croaked.

'I noticed you guys rushing out the door so I was a bit concerned.'

Lance glanced at Stephanie. 'I needed a cigarette so I asked Stephanie to come with me. She was not feeling the best so I said some fresh air would be good.'

Bruno folded his arms as Lance walked over to him.

'We have not met properly... I'm Lance and you're Bruno...'

'That's right.' He glared at Lance. 'It's good you came tonight. Are you into dancing?'

'I'm willing to give anything a try.'

Bruno nodded. 'When you've had that smoke you should come and dance.'

Lance touched his pocket. 'Changed my mind, can't find my cigarettes must have left them in the car. It's chilly out here. We're thinking of calling it a night. I think Stephanie is feeling a little bit tired.'

'Are you sure? There's still plenty more dancing to come.'

'Thank you but we'll give it a miss,' Lance replied in a stern voice.

'Okay, thanks for coming. I'll let Anton know you've gone. See you at the next class, Stephanie.'

Bruno left.

'Did you see his snake tattoo? I was thinking of getting a crow tattoo a while ago. Good old Adelaide Crows, they're the footy team to follow.'

Stephanie ignored his comment. 'Lance, why do you want to leave?'

'Why do you want to be around drug dealers?'

'I never said he was a drug dealer. The girls are probably making it all up.' Stephanie started to walk away from Lance.

'Come on, Stephanie. Don't be like that.'

'Be like what?'

'Defending Anton. He's in love with himself and flirts with all the women so they'll fall in love with him.'

'I'm upset that you used me as an excuse to leave,' she huffed, folding her arms.

'And I don't think Anton is in love with himself, Lance… You're just jealous of him.'

'I am not,' laughed Lance. 'I think you're just in love with him but you don't want to admit it.'

Stephanie took a deep breath. 'Leave me alone. I don't want to talk to you anymore.'

'This is silly, Stephanie. How are you going to get home?'

'I'll call a taxi.'

'But I can drive you.'

'I don't want to go with you.'

'I'm not leaving you here with these druggies.'

'Leave me alone, Lance.'

'Fine! I'll call you tomorrow,' Lance said as he walked off.

What a nightmare… Should I go back and say goodbye to Anton? No I need to leave. Stephanie sighed, so much had happened. She pulled out her mobile and called Emma.

'Em, can you talk now?'

'Of course, what's the matter?'

'I need help. I need to get out of here.'

'Where are you?'

'I just left the dance function. I'm standing out the front.'

'What happened?'

'I'm not feeling that great so I left.' Stephanie took a few slow paces down the street.

'Not feeling great? Did you eat something funny?'

'Em … I think I have feelings for Anton.'

'Ohhh I see, why did you leave then?' Emma asked.

'I didn't get to talk to him, I – '

'Well that's not a reason to leave, go back inside and try to…'

'I … I can't.'

'Why not? What's going on? Go back in there and ask Anton to dance.'

Stephanie looked around, she wanted to make sure she was alone and that no one was listening. She breathed heavily into the phone. 'Some of the girls were taking drugs tonight. I'm scared Em…'

Emma gasped. 'In that case I'm coming to get you now! Text me the address and I'll be there soon.'

'Thanks heaps.'

Chapter Thirty-One

Stephanie shivered as the wind blew her hair. Brushing it from her face she sighed.

'You're still here? I thought you were leaving.'

Stephanie turned around. 'Oh, hi Bruno. Yeah, my lift is coming soon.'

'I thought you were going home with Lance.'

'There was a change of plans.' Stephanie bit her lip.

Bruno's eyes gleamed as he walked closer. 'You seem like a smart girl. You should come back upstairs and wait. It's not a nice place out on the streets. You never know who might be around.'

Stephanie's hands started to tremble as he stood beside her. 'My lift shouldn't be long,' she muttered.

'You're a stubborn girl.'

Stephanie caught a wisp of his smoky breath.

'Just kidding. Guess I'll have to stay here too.' Placing his hand into his pocket Bruno looked up into the night sky. 'I like looking at the moon, it lights up the sky.' Stephanie bit her nail as he gave her a sideways glance.

'A long time ago, where Anton and I grew up, the people had great respect for the moon. We would have never dreamt of coming to live in Australia. Have you ever visited Peru?'

Again, she caught his smoky breath.

'I've never visited Peru,' she replied, 'but I recently read a book called *The Undiscovered Worlds of Peru*.'

Bruno's eyes narrowed as he pursed his lip.

'Peru is a place everyone should visit.'

'I'm sure it would be an interesting place to visit. I read about the Incas in the book.'

'My people.' Bruno's cold glare was intense. Stephanie shivered. She wanted to change the subject. 'I've always lived here. Both of my parents were born in Australia.'

Bruno tossed his head, 'Ha, I don't know where my parents are.'

'Did you lose touch with them?' Stephanie asked.

'My mother was born in Spain and my father was born in South America but I think they're dead.'

'Dead?' Stephanie whispered.

'Yes, dead! There are plenty of kidnappings and murders in South America.'

'Oh....' Stephanie nearly lost her balance as she leaned onto one foot.

'Are you okay?' Bruno frowned.

'I just lost my balance. I'm not used to wearing high heels.' Stephanie quickly covered her mouth as she coughed.

'You don't look well. Your skin is so pale,' Bruno commented. 'Hey ... you like trying new things, right?'

'Not sure what you mean...'

Bruno's hand came out of his pocket. 'You might want to try this?'

HONK!

'Is that your friend?' Bruno frowned.

Stephanie could see Emma waving to her from the car on

the other side of the road. Bruno quickly put his hand back in his pocket.

'Yeah, that's Emma. I better go.'

She hurried over to the car and opened the door without even looking back.

'Who's that guy?' Emma asked.

'Anton's brother, Bruno.'

'Anton's brother? Why was he with you?'

'I'm not sure. He just appeared from nowhere.'

'He looked kind of strange,' Emma glanced in her rear vision mirror.

'Bruno just said I should go back upstairs but I wanted to wait outside. I knew you wouldn't be long.'

'You should play it safe, Steph.'

Stephanie ignored her comment. 'Strange in what way?'

'I dunno … just the way he was standing.'

'He came out earlier when Lance was there too…'

'Huh? Who's Lance?' Emma took another glance in her mirror.

'He's just a friend who came along tonight. But he went home not long ago … '

'Mmm, I'm totally confused.'

Stephanie sighed. 'He offered to drive me home but I didn't want to go with him.'

'Well, I'm glad to hear that. You can't trust anyone these days.'

'He left because he didn't want to be around … drugs.'

'Yeah, and neither should you, or anyone for that matter.'

'Em,' Stephanie groaned. 'I don't want to talk about it anymore. It's Anton I can't get out of my head.'

'Do you think he likes you?'

'I'm not sure. His eyes sparkle when he looks at me … he's

winked at me quite a few times as well.'

'He's flirting, that's a good sign! Hang on … he might be a player. Does he do that to all the girls?'

'I'm not sure really, that's what he does to me.'

'Come on, think about when you've seen him dance with other girls.'

Stephanie shrugged. 'I know all the girls are in love with him.'

'That's interesting…'

'Look, all I know is … '

'Know what Stephanie?'

'I think my feelings for him have been building up over time…'

'Why do you think that?' Emma asked.

'It happened tonight when I saw all the girls dancing around him … I wished it was me … I wanted him to talk to – '

'But you said he didn't talk to you?' Emma interrupted.

'I think that was because all the girls were around him and he was too busy.'

'Hmmm, what are we going to do about this?'

Stephanie breathed deeply. 'I just need to know.'

'Need to know what?'

'I'm so confused,' Stephanie admitted.

'About what?'

'Anton!'

'REPEAT! What are we going to do about this… I can see it's really worrying you.'

'Yeah, it is. It's driving me crazy. He looks at me as if he's interested but then the next minute he's so cold… I'm not sure if he's playing games.'

'STEPHANIE! You don't need this… You've been through so much already.'

'What am I going to do?'

'There are two options. You either leave the dance school or ask him directly. He still may not tell you the truth though… I think he would have asked you for a coffee or something if he really likes you.'

'But Em, he's my teacher.'

'So what! If he likes you enough, he would … '

'Why would he notice me?' Stephanie asked.

'Because you're a beautiful person. You're kind, caring and loving.'

'But I'm not like the other girls.'

'Even more reason to like you! Stop beating yourself up, Steph. Personally, I think Daniel is the way to go. He was so well mannered. He's a lawyer and he has eyes to die for. Why not wait and see what happens with him?'

'I just can't stop thinking about Anton,' Stephanie snapped in frustration. 'There's something about him, some kind of mystery.'

Emma wrinkled her nose. 'Come on Steph, you think about it. Anton knows he's good looking and can charm any woman. He dances with girls all the time. That's his job. How can you trust someone like that? And now you've mentioned drugs too?'

'I don't know what to do, I'm so confused,' Stephanie looked out the window as they drove along the shopping strip.

'Look, I have to agree with this Lance guy… If drugs are involved, I think you should clearly step away…'

'I have to be true to myself, Em.'

'What do you mean by that?'

'I have to ask him. Then I can decide.'

The car pulled onto the driveway.

'Well, it's your decision in the end, but be careful. You don't really know him. I'm just saying this because I care...'

'I have to know, Em. I think I'll pay him a visit. Then I can see how he reacts,'

'If that's what you think is best, you know I'll support you with any decision. That's what friends are for. See you on Monday,' she smiled in approval.

'Thanks so much, Em,' Stephanie leaned over and hugged her friend.

Standing on the driveway, she waved Emma goodbye.

Hopefully by visiting Anton tomorrow I will find out some answers...

Stephanie gasped. Something was moving in the bushes.

'Who's there?' she whispered. Soft fur brushed her leg as it made its way across the path.

'Damn cat, scared me half to death, I nearly tripped over you,' she said aloud.

'Maybe you should be scared.'

Stephanie turned around and gasped heavily again. 'What do you want, Lance?'

'I followed you home in my taxi.'

'Why?' Stephanie frowned. 'I told you to leave me alone.'

'I saw that Bruno guy come back as I was about to leave. I needed to see that you got home safely.'

'Look Lance, please leave me alone. I don't want to see you again.'

Lance leaned closer to Stephanie. 'But what have I done? I thought you wanted to get to know each other. You invited me tonight.'

'Lance, I don't want this. Please just leave me alone ...'

'Stephanie, I didn't mean to upset you. Maybe I can take you out for coffee tomorrow?'

Why is he not getting the message? she thought.

'There's someone else,' she snapped.

'What did you say?' Lance asked.

'There's someone else!'

'Anton?'

'No … just someone else.'

'Who?'

Stephanie had to think quickly. 'Someone I met on a dating app.'

'A dating app? Are you kidding me?'

'Yeah, it's pretty serious too.'

'Cool. Don't bother calling me again, Stephanie.' Lance's attitude suddenly changed. 'You're just like all the other girls, you know that? Leading me on, calling me to come pick you up all the time, inviting me to a dance. My ex never knew what she wanted either!'

'Please stop shouting,' Stephanie whispered.

'I'm not shouting. You know … I bet you wouldn't notice a nice guy even if he was standing under your nose.'

'You're … you're so rude.'

'Me rude? Look at how you've treated me tonight. I was just looking out for you.'

'Whatever, Lance. I'm going inside.'

'Fine!' He threw his hands up into the air.

Stephanie got out her keys and headed for the door.

Quickly entering the house, Stephanie locked herself inside and ran to the window to peer through the crack in the curtain. She could see Lance getting into his yellow taxi.

Stephanie began to tremble, she wondered if she should tell someone about Lance. Was this the first time he had been to her house uninvited? She had seen a completely different side to him tonight. *That's what I get for trying to make friends with a complete stranger*, she thought. *But did I lead him on? Surely not!* She watched him as he just sat in the car. He had not turned on his lights or started the engine. She knew she had never liked Lance in a romantic sense, only ever as a friend. Emma's words repeated in her mind.

'*You can't trust anyone these days …* '

Stephanie sighed in relief as she watched the taxi leave. Her thoughts quickly turned back to Anton.

Tomorrow I hope to find some more answers. I need to talk to him. I'm going to take the risk …

Chapter Thirty-Two

Stephanie now carried her dance bag wherever she went, as if it were permanently attached to her shoulder, All she could think about was Anton.

'Mum, I'm off to meet a friend.'

'Stephanie, I didn't get to ask you how last night went?'

Stephanie shrugged. 'It was okay.'

'Did you get to dance much?'

'Not really, sorry, I'm running late,' Stephanie said as she kissed her mother on the cheek. 'Talk to you later, love you.'

A strange thought entered Stephanie's mind as she left the house. *Was Anton the tall dark figure Madam Farrell had seen in the crystal ball?*

Stephanie's hands began to tremble as she pushed the door of the dance school. To her relief, it opened. Music was playing inside. Stephanie took a deep breath, grabbed the railing and climbed the stairs.

Anton stood behind the desk.

'Hi Stephanie, this is a surprise.'

'I was just in the area and I wanted to tell you I'm sorry I didn't get to say goodbye last night.' She bit her nail and looked into his eyes.

Anton nodded.

'Don't worry, I noticed you.' He smiled.

'You did?' she gasped.

'Yes, I did. You looked lovely but I didn't get to dance with you. You left early.'

'I had to.'

'Never mind, let's not waste time now. I guess this is what you have come for. Hurry up and put on your dance shoes.'

Reaching into her bag, she pulled out her dance shoes and put them on her feet.

He took her hand, guiding her onto the dance floor.

'Don't say a word,' Anton whispered, placing his finger to his lips.

The two dancers gently swayed in the middle of the dance floor as the bright beam from the fluorescent light caught Stephanie's figure, casting a delicate shadow upon the wooden floorboards.

Listening to the music, Stephanie allowed Anton to lead her movements. Rotating her hips in time with his, she danced the Salsa steps. The movements were easy and loose, and although swaying her hips was something she was once afraid of, this was no longer the case.

'Stephanie, I love the way you move your hips.'

'Thanks.' She smiled shyly. 'Anton, I need to ask you something. Are you …'

'Am I what?'

'Are you … interested in me at all, like, romantically?'

'Steph … I'm your dance teacher. I'm much older than you.'

'But I've been in a relationship with an older guy before.'

'Stephanie … let's just concentrate on the steps.'

Stephanie sighed. Anton did not understand what she had been dealing with, the recent loss of Andrew and the struggle to get out of bed every morning. Dancing with him had now become her life.

'But Anton ...' she muttered as he continued to dance. Her weary body gently swayed as he led her into the next step. Trying to catch his gaze she lost balance and the sole of her shoe slipped against the floor.

'Ah!' she shrieked.

'What happened? Did you hurt yourself?'

'My foot ...' She leaned over to rub her ankle.

Anton placed his hand on her shoulder. Stephanie stared wildly into his eyes.

'Steph ... some things are just not meant to be,' he said quietly as he offered her his other hand.

Stephanie tried to fight back the hot tears forming in her eyes. Gently dropping a kiss on her forehead Anton then led her off the dance floor.

'Sit down and rest that foot. I've got something to help you,' Anton offered. Turning his back, he switched off the dance music and left the room.

Looking down at her feet she noticed her toes had changed colour as the black straps dug deeper into her soft skin. Taking off her dance shoes, the colour seeped back into her feet. A teardrop landed on her lips as a salty taste entered her mouth. Wiping her eyes, the black mascara smudged onto her hands.

Pins and needles ran up the back of Stephanie's legs. She looked over at the staircase, wondering if she should make an exit. Struggling to stand, she took a deep breath and faced the stairs. Stephanie paused to rub her aching leg. She gasped, someone was breathing on the back of her neck.

'Anton? Is that you?'

'You look in pain.'

Someone pushed her back onto the couch. Stephanie looked up to see Anton standing over her. He held out a glass of water.

'I didn't mean to scare you. Here, take this.'

'What's this?' she hesitated. Tiny silver specks started to appear in front of her eyes.

'Trust me, just take it! The pain will go away.'

Anton handed Stephanie a white tablet. Her hand trembled as she accepted his offer.

'Go on. What are you waiting for?'

Closing her eyes, she allowed the tablet to slip down her throat.

Shit, thought Stephanie. *What have I done?*

'Is she still conscious?'

Bruno entered the dance studio.

'Quick, let's move her into the back room.'

'No! You can't do that.'

'Shut up, Anton! I'll do what I like,' he snapped.

Stephanie gasped as Bruno grabbed her under her arm.

'Grab the other side, Anton.'

'What are you doing? Let go of me!'

'Shut up!' Bruno shouted.

Her legs slid across the polished floorboards as her head fell backwards.

'Anton, we don't want anyone to walk in and see her lying on the couch - not good for business. Now go and grab her shoes, make yourself useful.'

The door slammed closed. Lying flat on her back, Stephanie

could not move. Her legs ached and her neck felt stiff. Sharp pain shot up her back. She wondered how the enjoyment of dance could have led her down such a destructive path.

Chapter Thirty-Three

Her neck rubbed on the rough carpeted floor as she tried to take deep breaths. She squinted, closing her eyes tightly and then re-opening them. Something shiny against the wall caught her eye. The object was sticking out from behind the cupboard. It was attached to a black handle.

Stephanie gasped. It was a butcher's knife. She rocked her body from side to side and managed to roll onto her side. The clock on the wall ticked loudly.

Another sharp pain shot up the side of Stephanie's arm. Her muscles tightened.

The door flung open.

'Should we put this girl's body in here too?' Anton asked.

'No Anton, she's dead. I gave her the drugs last night. No, actually, you gave her the pills,' snapped Bruno.

Anton threw his hands into the air. 'Who cares who killed her off. Let's put her in the boot of the car … Hang on, let's wrap the body in black plastic first.'

The two brothers stood in the middle of the room. Stephanie shut her eyes and held her breath.

'Actually … ' Bruno pondered. 'We'll do that when we get rid of it tonight. Shut the door, just in case anyone in the dance school walks past. We don't want them to see that body lying on the floor over there. What was her name again?'

'Stephanie. The dead girl is Eve.'

Stephanie gasped. She could not believe Eve was dead.

'Did you have a fling with both girls?' Bruno started to laugh.

'I never cared about them, only their money,' Anton grumbled. 'Eve was getting a little too friendly last night. When I told her I didn't want anything to do with her, she threatened to tell the police about us. It had to be done.'

Tears rolled down Stephanie's cheeks. Anton was nothing but a drug dealing murderer.

'Enough chat, let's get to work. Don't you have a private lesson soon?'

'Soon, it's with Tam. She's in love with me too. It's all good, I think I have that situation under control at the moment.'

Stephanie's thoughts turned to Zara and the other girls. *Anton gave them pills last night,* she thought. *What if they've been murdered too?*

'Do you think we could get Tam onto the drugs too?'

'All in good time, brother. Come on, let's put Eve's body in the car.'

The door slammed shut. Hot tears continued to stream down Stephanie's cheeks. She could hear footsteps outside the door. She wondered if anyone would realise that she was missing.

The door flung open again. It was Helena.

'Stephanie! What have they done to you?'

'Helena! Thank God! I have to get out of here. They'll be back soon. They've … they've killed Eve.'

Helena gasped and her eyes started to water. 'I didn't think it would lead to this. I wish they had never got into the drug business. I know it was a way for them to make quick money but the trouble it has gotten them into.'

'Helena, get me out of here.'

'I'm going to get help. I'll be back.'

'No, please stay! Don't leave me!'

Helena left the room shutting the door behind her.

Stephanie closed her eyes. At least someone knew she was there.

The phone started to ring. Anton and Bruno were still outside with the body.

Rocking back and forth, Stephanie used her arms to help her lever herself to an upright position. Her head was thumping as if someone had punched her in the face. She needed to be strong and do this.

Placing her palms down onto the carpet she pushed herself up onto her feet, wobbling back and forth she tried to regain her balance. Once she was steady on her feet, she took a giant step and leaned towards the table where the phone was still ringing. Her hand trembled as she stretched out to grab the receiver.

'Please, help me,' she whispered into the phone.

The phone line was dead.

Stephanie heard a voice in the hallway. It was Bruno.

'I think the phone was ringing.'

'I'll check the back room,' Anton hissed.

The phone fell from Stephanie's grip as she plunged onto the floor.

The door flung open.

'Stephanie, can you hear me?' Anton sat next to her.

'Did the phone ring?' Anton's musky aftershave drifted under Stephanie's nose.

'Yes,' she mumbled.

'What did you say? I can't hear you?' Anton leaned in closer.

'Yes.'

'Damn Steph! Stop stressing. I only gave you a Panadol to relieve the pain. You know I wouldn't hurt you.' Anton stared into Stephanie's eyes. 'You must trust me. Bruno and I have had a tough life. That's why it wouldn't work between us. You don't want to get involved with me. You're different from the other girls.' He winked at Stephanie. 'But whatever you do, don't speak to Bruno.'

'Did the phone ring?' Bruno barged into the room. He had a black hooded jacket on that covered his dark hair.

'Yeah, it did bro.'

'Shit! I think it would have been Marco about the deal. He said he was going to ring today.' Bruno put his hand on Anton's shoulder. 'Tape her mouth.'

'No!' Anton pushed Bruno's hand off his shoulder. 'She's injured her foot. There's no chance of her running away.'

Bruno gave Anton a sideways glance. 'Hey man, I'm the older brother and the boss here.' He made his way to the cupboard and walked back with a roll of black tape. 'Hold her head while I tape her mouth.'

Stephanie's head rested in the palms of Anton's hands. She began to struggle as the masking tape was plastered tightly onto her lips. The pressure was intense. She breathed through her nostrils.

Anton showed no emotion.

'Now, should we tie her hands up?'

'No need for that.' Anton gently rested her head on the ground.

'Why not?' Bruno demanded. 'Anton! If she tries to escape it will be so much harder for her. We can't risk her getting away and squealing to the cops.'

Anton looked at Stephanie.

Bruno frowned. 'Anton, don't tell me you have feelings for this girl?'

'I don't have feelings for her. I just know Stephanie is weak, no athlete for sure.'

'Good. I should have known she's not your type.' Bruno said as he put the tape back in the cupboard. 'You had me worried for a moment, Anton. You know we can't have feelings for any girls. We want them all to love us. If not, we'll lose the business.' He rested his hand on Anton's shoulder. 'Us brothers need to stick together. Remember the last girl who got close to me?'

'No?' Anton stood back.

'Had to strangle her with my belt,' Bruno sniggered. 'Let's go. Switch off the light.'

Only a tiny bit of light from the hallway seeped under the door. Outside, Stephanie could hear a female voice.

'Tam, how has your day been?' Anton greeted her as she walked into the studio.

'Sunday always seems to be busy in the nail shop. You get so many complaining customers.'

'Yes, people seem to complain all the time. Do you like my new haircut?' Anton asked.

'I like your hair short,' Tam giggled. 'I thought something was different.'

'I like fringes that go off to the side.'

'Fringes are good,' Tam said.

Anton walked over to the mirror. 'Look at me I need to have a shave. Tuesday and Friday are my shave days.'

'Anton, stop looking in the mirror. Let's dance. That's what I want to do with my life. I want to become a professional dancer. Have you always wanted to dance?'

'My mother encouraged me to dance. She loved dancing and

said when I was little I used to clap my hands every time I saw someone dancing.'

'My family left Vietnam so I could dance. I'm prepared to train hard. Thanks for letting me have a lesson on Sundays. It's so lovely dancing with you.'

Anton began to laugh. 'We're going to practice the Cha, Cha today. We need to work on your New Yorkers. How is the tummy toning going?'

'I went to the gym on Friday night … 'Tam hesitated. 'I have an idea … '

'What's that?'

'Maybe we could go to the gym together?'

Anton folded his arms. 'I'm your dance teacher. I'll leave that to your personal trainer.'

'What days do you go to the gym?' Tam asked.

'Whenever I can get there,' Anton said as he turned to admire himself in the mirror. . 'I need to work on building my muscles. Strength is so important for a male dancer.'

'Sooo … are we going to start dancing?'

'That's what we're here for,' Anton laughed. 'Or maybe we could talk about entertainment. You could entertain me. Just kidding, back to business. I'll put the music on.'

Stephanie could hear the music playing.

'No, you're not doing that right,' Anton said. 'You need to match my frame. Try again.'

Stephanie closed her eyes and listened to Anton's voice.

'You need to keep that movement in the hips. I'm going to turn off the music until you get the steps right.'

'I'm trying my best,' Tam said.

'When performing the Cha Cha you need to be fast and cheeky and have a forward and backward action. It's important you understand this. Jive is a different style altogether. Bouncy with high kicks but that's for another lesson. We're concentrating on the Cha Cha today.'

Stephanie closed her eyes and pictured herself dancing. *I need to distract myself,* she thought.

'That's all for tonight, Tam. Please don't leave your top in the ladies toilet again. Don't make it the third time in two weeks.'

Tam started to giggle. 'Anton, this place is like a second home. I bring everything with me. I even brought my toothbrush.'

'Are you serious?'

Tam nodded.

'Go home and practice the steps.' Anton changed the subject.

'I will…I'm going to write what I learnt in my dance journal.'

'You need to have discipline if you're going to get anywhere.'

Tam bit her lip.

'Success only happens for those who want it badly. You need to stand out from the rest and focus on your goals,' Anton said sternly.

'I'm not quite sure what you mean?'

'It starts with the training, hours and hours after each dance lesson. I want you to feel like you can barely walk. We need to finish the lesson now.' Anton said.

'I have to change my shoes before I leave. I can't wear my dance shoes on the street. I'm looking forward to getting my driver's licence so I don't have to catch the tram or walk home.'

Anton raised an eyebrow. 'It's good to have your licence.'

'Could you maybe drive me home?' she asked.

'Sorry Tam, I can't. I've got a lot to do. I'll see you next week.'

'Okay … bye Anton.'

Stephanie opened her eyes, how she longed to see the daylight.

'Has she gone now?' Bruno asked

'Yeah, she's gone.'

'Let's go and get rid of the body. I think we'll lock up now, Anton. We'll come back for Stephanie later.'

She tried to scream but couldn't move her lips.

'Where are we going to dump the body?' Anton asked.

'I was thinking near the Yarra River somewhere. We'll decide when we're driving. Let's go.'

Chapter Thirty-Four

The back door shut.

Stephanie did not have much time. As she lay on her back, she rocked her body from side to side. With a great amount of effort, she managed to roll herself onto her left side. Curling into a little ball she tucked one foot underneath, the other foot ached. Using the little strength she had left she managed to sit up. She knew she had to take it one step at a time.

Breathing deeply through her nostrils she tried to relax her shoulders. Her whole body trembled as she heard the door open again.

'We should put her in the car as well, that's a much better idea!' Bruno shouted.

Stephanie fell back onto the hard floor as the door flung open.

The two men stood over her.

'She's not dead. We can't put her in the boot of the car,' Anton said. 'Eve's in there anyway.'

'Guess we'll just have to sit her in the back seat Anton.' Bruno's eyes glared down onto Stephanie's body and then to her mouth.

'We can't leave that tape on her mouth if she's sitting up in the car, that will look suspicious. Hold her up a minute, Anton.'

Anton's hands gripped Stephanie's body as Bruno ripped the tape off her lips. Stephanie trembled and closed her eyes. Moving the tip of her tongue down gently onto her lip, she could taste blood. Taking a deep breath, she breathed through her mouth again. Something cold and sharp rested against her neck.

'If you scream I'll cut your throat,' Bruno whispered into her ear.

Stephanie saw the light hit the silver blade as it was removed from her throat.

'Anton, carry her out while I lock up.'

He nodded and began to carry her. She let her arms and legs hang over his arms as they supported her weak body. Stephanie did not want to look at his face. She sighed as he carried her out the back exit. The moon lit up the dark sky. She could see a black Jeep that was parked in the shadows. There were no other cars around. The wind blew Stephanie's hair as Anton rested her on the ground and opened the door.

'Don't say a word,' he whispered.

Anton placed her on the back seat and shut the door.

'Right, ready to go.' Bruno put the keys into the ignition and started the engine.

Resting her head against the window, she did not dare speak.

'Damn Anton, I need to get some petrol. There's a service station just up the road.'

The Jeep turned into the petrol station.

'You stay here,' Bruno snapped.

As the door opened, Stephanie smelt the petrol fumes.

'I think I'm going to be sick, Anton,' Stephanie muttered.

Anton turned around in his seat to face her.

'Listen to me,' he said. 'This is your chance to escape. You don't have long. If you don't get out of here, Bruno is going to kill you. You know too much.' He took off his seatbelt. 'I'm going to tell Bruno I need to go to the bathroom. I'll leave the door unlocked. When Bruno goes to pay, get out of the car and run for your life.'

'But Anton – '

'There are no buts, just do it,' he ordered.

Anton opened the door and then slammed it shut. Stephanie peered out the window. She could see the two brothers talking. Bruno was frowning but Anton looked calm. Turning away from his brother, Anton started to make his way towards the building. Bruno then looked at the petrol pump meter and started to walk towards the building too.

NOW!

Grabbing the handle and pushing open the door, she slid herself off the seat. Stephanie allowed her feet to touch the ground. She had to move quickly even though she was barely able to stand.

Along the pavement in the dark she hobbled. Stephanie did not know where she was going. The cold wind whipped against her cheeks. She knew if Bruno found her she would have no hope. The headlights of a passing car flashed across her body as it did a U-turn in the middle of the road. Stopping at a side street, she leaned against a pole. There was a second-hand car yard across the road, Fitzroy Car Sales and in the distance she could see a red, orange and green sign, a food store. She limped her way passed various closed shops making a desperate rush for the food store.

'Hey you! You got a cigarette?' a woman called out.

Stephanie continued to walk.

'Stupid girl!'

Stephanie remained focused as she was nearly at the food store. Pushing open the door, she stumbled to the counter.

'I need to use your phone. It's an emergency. Lock the door, please!'

The dark skinned man stared back at her. 'Are you okay, miss? Your lips are bleeding.'

'Please, just give me the phone,' she panted.

The man handed her the phone and then went to lock the doors.

She called Emma's number.

'Please pick up the phone, Em.'

'Steph?'

'Em, I'm in trouble, I was nearly kidnapped.'

'What! Where are you? I'm coming to get you.'

'I'm in Fitzroy at a 7 Eleven.'

'Where? Which 7 Eleven?'

'It's near Fitzroy Car Sales.'

'I'll be there as fast as I can!' Emma hung up.

Silver specks floated in front of Stephanie's eyes.

She sat on the floor and then everything went black.

Chapter Thirty-Five

'She's awake!' Emma shouted.

Standing in front of Stephanie were her parents and Emma.

'What happened?' She asked as she lay in the bed.

Her mother took her hand.

Stephanie blinked. 'Mum … where am I?'

'You're in hospital, Stephanie. You were in trouble and called Emma from the food store.'

Stephanie rubbed her eyes.

'When you're feeling better we want to hear what happened,' her mother muttered. 'Your lips …' She shook her head with watery eyes.

'Who kidnapped you, Steph? Was it Anton?' Emma whispered.

'Yes … '

'What happened?'

Stephanie bit her swollen lip and looked at her mother for support.

'Darling, it's safe in here,' her mother squeezed her hand. 'The shop assistant rang the ambulance and contacted the police straight away.' She gave a gentle nod. 'You'll need to talk to the police later, but for now we need to know what happened.'

'Police!' Stephanie sat up in her bed.

'Just rest for the moment, darling,' her mother reassured.

Stephanie groaned and lay back onto the pillow.

'Did he hurt you?' Emma leaned in closer.

'Yes … well, he didn't really hurt me. It was Bruno.'

'Why were your lips bleeding?' Emma asked.

Stephanie's eyes started to water. 'They taped my mouth so I couldn't speak.'

Her mother let go of her hand and sank onto the chair. She couldn't believe what she was hearing.

'All I remember was going to see Anton … I hurt my foot so I sat down for a bit … he brought me a glass of water and a tablet to help me feel better … then I …' she hesitated.

'Then what?' her mother asked.

'I was taken into the back room. Bruno grabbed the black tape and … ' Stephanie swallowed.

'Are you okay?' Emma snorted.

'I just felt a sudden pain in my side.'

Emma placed her hand on Stephanie's forehead. 'You feel hot.'

'I was frightened Emma,' Stephanie whispered. 'What happens if they come back for me?'

'That won't happen,' her dad said as he walked closer to the bed and rested his hand on her pillow. 'These men must be found, charged and put in prison.'

A tear rolled down Stephanie's cheek as Emma handed her a tissue. She dabbed it on her eyes. A lady in a white uniform walked into the room.

'Excuse me for interrupting but the doctor wanted me to let you know that he feels Stephanie will be fine to leave. Doctor Henry will write up a report about her condition. The police will be contacting you at home.'

'Thank you,' her mother said.

'You're welcome.' The nurse nodded and left the room.

Stephanie looked at her parents. 'Mum, Dad I'm scared.' Another tear rolled down her cheek.

Emma stepped back as her mother made her way over to the bed.

'Don't worry, we'll be with you,' she said as she reached for her hand. 'Your clothes are on the chair. We'll leave the room while you get ready. Take your time.' She kissed Stephanie's forehead gently and smiled then walked out of the room, holding her husband's hand tightly.

'Can I get you another tissue?' Emma asked.

Stephanie shook her head.

'Steph, I've been thinking. Does Bruno or Anton have a tattoo?'

Stephanie shrugged. 'I overheard some of the girls from the dance school chatting about Anton having a bird tattoo.'

'What about Bruno?'

'Yes Bruno has a …' Stephanie hesitated, 'a snake tattoo.' She suddenly gasped. 'Surely not!'

'We have to find out if he's linked to Andrew's death.' Emma grabbed her jacket.

'Do you really think it could be him?'

'I'm going to drive to the dance school,' Emma said sternly.

'Don't do that, Emma! It could be dangerous.'

'I'll be in touch. Don't worry about me.'

Stephanie closed her eyes. The echoing sound of footsteps in the corridor was the only noise that carried into the room.

'Tape her mouth, I might take the knife too … '

Stephanie could visualise the horrid scene.

Throwing off the bed sheets, she grabbed her jeans and pulled them over her lanky legs. On went her top and then her jumper. 'Time to go, I'm ready,' she mouthed as she left the hospital room and made her way into the corridor.

'Home is where the heart is,' her mother reassured as they entered the front door of the house.

Stephanie breathed a sigh of relief, she was glad to be home.

'Here we are, dear,' her mother continued. 'Your father will get things organised.'

Stephanie shuffled past the coffee table. Touching her neck, she remembered the cold sensation that had rested against it for only a few seconds. Her thin body sunk onto the couch.

'I bet you're glad to be home,' her mother said as she relaxed on the couch and reached her arm around her daughter.

'I'm so tired and sore,' Stephanie touched her lips.

'They look very inflamed sweetheart.'

'I could taste blood and he … '

'What happened?' her mother leaned in closer.

'He put a knife to my neck.'

'Darling, here, give me a proper hug.'

Stephanie held her mother tightly. 'I'm trying not to think about it Mum,' she muttered. 'I'm still in so much pain.'

'Maybe you should go and lie down on your bed for a while. Close your eyes and rest your back. Your father and I aren't going anywhere.'

Stephanie sighed. 'Thanks mum.'

Closing her bedroom door, her hands trembled.

The heavy rain was beating on her bedroom window as she sat on the bed. Reaching into her pocket, Stephanie pulled out her mobile and rang Emma.

'Emma's phone! Leave a message!'

Stephanie groaned. Placing her finger on the redial button, she let it call again.

'Hi Steph.'

'Emma, why didn't you answer? I was getting worried.'

'Sorry, I didn't hear the phone. Everything is locked up here at the dance school. No sign of anyone. It all seems a bit strange – '

'That is strange,' Stephanie interrupted. 'They usually would be open today.'

Emma breathed deeply into the phone. 'I'm not sure what's going on... I'm guessing the police may come some time. Anyway I'm going to leave now. I don't want to say much because you never know who might be listening. Just rest, we can't do anything at the moment. I'll talk to you soon.' Emma hung up.

Placing her mobile next to her, Stephanie relaxed her head back onto the pillow and covered herself with the sheets. Listening to the rain, she gently closed her eyes.

Buzzzzz!

Stephanie grabbed her phone. The bright light from the screen shone into her eyes. Message from Anton.

DON'T FORGET ME ...

Three months later...

Stephanie watched her new teacher Vicky demonstrate the Jive steps. Her bubbly personality and passion for dance was contagious.

The first step taught was the Rock Step involving a rocking hip action. Stephanie quickly fell in love with it, giving Emma a smile every time they practised it.

The new studio was closer to home and the people were so different compared to Dance Discovery. The dancers at Latin Diva Dance wore leggings and tops - not short skirts. They didn't make a fuss about which guys they danced with and focused on the steps - they just loved to dance.

The American Spin had become Stephanie's favourite step twirling around on the mark. It had been taught a few weeks into the dance lessons. She bopped on the spot, stopping now and then to catch her breath. Jive was a lively, energetic dance.

Stephanie wanted to learn more …

Epilogue

'Thanks, sir. We hope you enjoyed your flight. Welcome to Paris.'

'Sure did.'

Grabbing the black brief case, the two men briskly walked along the passageway with the other travellers.

'Keep walking and don't look back,' Bruno said.

The transparent sliding doors were only metres away. As they hit the beam they continued walking.

South America's most wanted criminals breathed a sigh of relief as they exited through the doors of Charles De Gaulle airport. The chilly breeze blew into their faces as car beams flickered across their clothes. The two brothers shook hands.

'Well, that went well. Welcome to your new home, brother.' Bruno patted Anton on the back. 'I'm meeting Ana in Provence. I'll call you in the next few weeks. And, remember, you're now responsible for this,' he whispered as he handed over the brief case. 'Our lives depend on it'.

Anton nodded. Bruno's black coat brushed against his arm.

'You have the address for the Moulin Rouge. It's located in Montmartre. Apparently you can't miss the place. There's a huge windmill out the front. Jean Paul will be waiting for you. Till we meet again, bro.'

Anton looked out onto the roadway. The full moon shone in the inky sky. Holding the handle of the leather case, he took a deep breath. Glancing at his gold watch, he realised it was only a matter of time.

Acknowledgments

Life is a journey of many ups and downs and I have so many people to thank.

Dance Demons has been a long journey and one of the hardest books I have written so far. It wouldn't be the book it is without the support, guidance and love from so many special and talented people.

Firstly I would like to thank Bryce Courtenay for encouraging me to start this story when I was a student in his final Masterclass. I wish you were here to see the final product.

To Jennifer Douglas, I would like to thank you for your support and guidance with polishing the *Dance Demons* story. Also to the cover designer, Wanissa Somsuphangsri, I am so thrilled with your work. A big thank you to Tara Wyllie, my fabulous editor who I have just discovered after writing three novels and now has assisted me in finding my writing voice and given me fresh eyes. Another huge thanks to Mark Zocchi for continuing to believe in me and for supporting every step I take in being a published author.

To Vicki and Dulcie, my first Jazz, Tap and Ballet teachers who taught me my first steps and a love for dance, I will always be grateful. For years, from the ages of 12 to 20, I spent time in your dance studio and you became my dance family.

Thanks also to Chris, Elena, Marcelle, Narelle, Cian, Emmanuel, Simone and Sarah, fellow classmates for sharing with me many years of laughter, dance and friendship.

To my new dance family developing my love of Latin dance, I thank you. Special thanks to the passionate and inspiring Cheryl who motivates me to follow my dreams and has helped me achieve my silver medal in Latin dance and now my gold medal in Cha Cha. Thanks also to Shane for helping me with this too. I would also like to mention Olga and thank her for sharing the love of dance and Carmen, Elia, Asanka, Jean, Jennie, Susan, Diego, Angela, Ursula, John, Dmitry, Dylan, Anne, Amanda, Skye, Stewart and Matt and all the people in my Latin dance family. I hope I have not forgotten anyone. And to all the dancers out there - never miss a chance to dance.

To my writing friends and readers who continue to support my journey and watch the growth and development of my writing, I am so grateful. And to my reading cheer squad Annie McCann, Sarah Clifton, Jessica Gill, Carolyn Ansky, Aditi Saha, Shirley Cuypers and Sue Anne, I hope you enjoy this book. Also to my new readers, thank you for your support. I hope you continue to read my books and follow my journey.

To my close family and friends, there is never a day that goes by that I do not feel blessed to have the most amazing group of people who love and support me and encourage me to do what I love. I would like to mention my Grandpa who at the age of 94 gets excited to hear about my latest book, thanks for your support. Also thank you Dee, Sash and Ashani for your friendship and being a listening ear always.

A big thank you to Mum and Dad for your constant encouragement, love, patience and support. Also I am so proud of my mum who has started Latin dancing at the age of 65 and also thankful to her for taking an interest and being involved always in my writing endeavours.

And finally, a special thank you to you, dear reader, for reading this book. It means so much to me as an author to have you spend the time and read my work.

I am blessed to be able to write about another passion of mine dance.

Remember, when dancing the Cha Cha, as in life, you sometimes have to take one step back in order to move two steps forward.

Dance Demons

Juliet M. Sampson

ISBN: 9781925367263		Qty
RRP	AU$ $19.99	.....
Postage within Australia	AU$5.00	.....
	TOTAL★ $_____	
	★ All prices include GST	

Name:..

Address: ....

....

Phone:...

Email: ....

Payment: ❏ Money Order ❏ Cheque ❏ MasterCard ❏ Visa

Cardholder's Name:...

Credit Card Number: ....

Signature:...

Expiry Date: ....

Allow 7 days for delivery.

Payment to: Marzocco Consultancy (ABN 14 067 257 390)
PO Box 12544
A'Beckett Street, Melbourne, 8006
Victoria, Australia
admin@brolgapublishing.com.au

BE PUBLISHED

Publish through a successful publisher.
Brolga Publishing is represented through:
• **National** book trade distribution, including sales,
marketing & distribution through **Macmillan Australia.**
• **International** book trade distribution to
    • The United Kingdom
    • North America
    • Sales representation in South East Asia
• **Worldwide e-Book distribution**

For details and inquiries, contact:
Brolga Publishing Pty Ltd
PO Box 12544
A'Beckett St VIC 8006

Phone: 0414 608 494
markzocchi@brolgapublishing.com.au
ABN: 46 063 962 443
(Email for a catalogue request)

www.ingramcontent.com/pod-product-compliance
Lightning Source LLC
Chambersburg PA
CBHW051536260626
47170CB00003B/957